Love's Misaligning Magic

Wildcrest Witches Book 2

HEATHER SILVIO

Panther Books

Panther Books: Worldwide.

Visit the author's website at https://www.heathersilvio.com
Contact the author at: heather@heathersilvio.com

Cover design by Sonia Freitas at Chloe Belle Arts
https://www.ChloeBelleArts.com

ISBN (Print) 9781951192150
ISBN (E-book) 9781951192167

BOOKS BY HEATHER SILVIO

WILDCREST WITCHES ROMANCE

Love's Misfiring Magic
Love's Misaligning Magic
Love's Misbehaving Magic

PARANORMAL TALENT AGENCY
(ALSO IN LARGE PRINT)

Lights, Camera, Action (Episode One)
Reset to One (Episode Two)
That's a Wrap (Episode Three)
An Unexpected Sequel (Episode Four)
Jumping the Shark (Episode Five)
The Season Finale (Episode Six)

COLLECTIONS

Paranormal Talent Agency Episodes 1-3 Collection
Paranormal Talent Agency Episodes 4-6 Collection
Paranormal Talent Agency Episodes 1-6 Collection

DOCTOR DANGER MYSTERIES

Hazard in Hawaii
Spirits in Savannah

NON-SERIES FICTION

Not Quite Famous: A Romantic Comedy of an Actress
on the Edge

Beyond the Abyss: Tales of the Supernatural

Courting Death

NONFICTION

Special Snowflake Syndrome: The Unrecognized
Personality Disorder Destroying the World

Happiness by the Numbers: 9 Steps to Authentic
Happiness

Stress Disorders: A Healing Path for PTSD

CHAPTER ONE

LAURA

Laura Harkin wondered if her realtor was showing her houses that didn't meet her criteria so they could spend more time together. Not that she objected, exactly. Aaron Wright was very easy to look at, with his messy brown hair, bright green eyes, and muscles outlined by his fitted blue pinstriped suit. He was too short for her, of course, but then most men were. It was hard for them to be taller when she was six feet tall in kitten heels.

"Is there anything you like about the house, Laura?"

It impressed her that he kept his tone even. The man had the patience of a saint. This was the fifth house that weekend they'd looked at. She wanted out of her rental, and after much hemming and hawing was finally moving forward with the search. Wildcrest, Nevada, being the map-dot-sized town it was, meant there wasn't a ton to choose from. She didn't want to wait for a new build, so it had to be used.

"Laura?"

She turned from the fireplace she was inspecting – *did I need a fireplace?* – and smiled, bright white teeth gleaming next to ruby red lipstick. "Apologies. I was thinking of the answer to your question."

"And?"

"There's quite a bit I like about the house," she admitted. "Single story, three bedrooms, quarter-acre lot."

"But?"

"But it's just not speaking to me." She lifted a shoulder in a shrug.

"I didn't know we needed a talking house."

Laura's laughter mingled with his. Although he was joking, in a town filled with witches, you never knew. Maybe she did want a talking house. "I want turnkey, though," she added.

"Naturally."

She listened for the sarcasm in the single word but didn't hear it. That was good. As a professional, it was important to her that the people she dealt with were also professional. Thus far, Aaron had exceeded those expectations.

If only he could find her the house of her dreams.

They walked together into the kitchen, which she acknowledged was renovated beautifully. "I like the white cabinets," she said, nodding when he made a note of it.

"What do you think of the island?"

Laura wrinkled her nose. It was bigger than she would prefer, and on wheels. She wanted a permanent island in her new kitchen. "Let me show you more of what I'd like to see."

All the witches in town possessed a magical inclination. This magic was an open secret, meaning none of the witches felt they needed to hide their abilities anymore. Not since the Las Vegas City Council officially recognized the existence of supernatural beings. But most still only displayed their powers around other witches.

Laura concentrated on the island and pictured in her head how she wanted it to appear. The top grew hazy, almost like a distant mirage, and then began to darken and change shape. Her magic was the ability to manipulate small amounts of matter. As she imagined the island with a butcher block top, not on wheels, and about half the size, it slowly took on that appearance.

"That's what I'm looking for."

"Very nice," Aaron said, circling the island, snapping a few pictures on his cellphone. He stopped beside her. "What's the most amount of matter you've reshaped?"

"The biggest was a car."

Such an awesome experience. She had wanted a new car when she graduated from college four years ago. They didn't have what she wanted, so she decided to experiment. She purchased a car that looked the closest and then manipulated it to look like what she pictured. Now she owned a bright-red sports car that appeared to be a 1968 Shelby Cobra, her favorite car (which she couldn't afford!)

"Wow, impressive. I've wondered what it would be like to have an active ability." He sounded almost wistful. "You know our family has more passive skills."

She placed her hand on his bicep. "Being so in touch with living beings is an amazing ability." Their eyes met, and she caught her breath when he took her hand in his.

"Thank you, Laura. We're thankful for what we have, too." He grinned and stepped away from her. "Although sometimes the animals can be quite chatty."

"What's it like, hearing what they say?" Laura was genuinely curious. Every witch could communicate in images and feelings with their familiar, or companion animal. That was where it ended for most of them. Aaron, however, could communicate with any animal. She couldn't imagine what that would be like.

Aaron's forehead crinkled. "It's hard to fully describe. It's more than what it sounds like you would hear with your familiar—"

"That's probably a good thing," she interrupted with a laugh. Her familiar was a tabby cat named Edward, the reincarnation of a great- great- great-uncle from the 1920s. He was a raggedy looking cat who preferred to go by Eddie, and missed everything about the Jazz Age.

"No doubt," he agreed. "I can almost understand them like they're speaking. It's like a universal translator in my head." He shrugged. "That's the best I can explain it."

"That sounds so interesting. To be able to communicate, to be that close…" She trailed off and walked out of the kitchen. No reason to consider being close to someone. Those thoughts would be unhelpful right now. Better to focus on the task at hand. "I also like bay windows. You can add that to the list."

"Noted."

"Let's head to the bedroom." Her face flushed at the words, and she hurried forward, the clicking of her heels barely covering the sound of Aaron's snort-laugh.

CHAPTER TWO

AARON

Aaron Wright hoped Laura hadn't heard him laugh. And snort-laughed, at that. He knew what she meant, though, and followed behind her without comment. Her hips swayed under a purple fitted tank dress that looked stunning next to her pale skin.

She turned when she reached the bedroom and he stopped up short, only about a foot from her. Her azure eyes widened theatrically and he stepped back.

"Sorry about that."

"That's okay," she stuttered before striding toward the master bathroom.

He opened his mouth to speak, and smiled instead.

Even though Laura was among the pickiest clients in his new real estate practice, he found that it didn't bother him. And luckily it didn't bother his sponsoring broker, who had a whole cadre of newbie realtors under her.

"I don't believe these renovations occurred at the same time," her voice echoed from the bathroom.

Aaron hurried to join her as she explained why the listing sheet from the seller's agent was inaccurate.

That was why Laura's pickiness didn't bother him. He delighted in spending time with her. She could be snarky, which was entertaining, but mostly he liked her intelligence. They'd spent hours together in the past month and he'd never once felt bored. That had to be a record.

But he wasn't dating her, so maybe just being friends was the difference. "What do you think of the closet size?" he asked.

She cocked a hip and together they stared into the cavernous space. It was huge, relative to the size of the bedroom. "This would do nicely."

"All of your clothes would fit?" He waggled his eyebrows.

"Hah, not hardly," she admitted. "But that's what dressers and guest bedroom closets are for."

Aaron chuckled and wrote, 'Master closet the size of a room.'

Laura stepped close and peered at his note. "I'd think you would have already made a note of that requirement."

"I'm emphasizing the requirement."

"Good, because some of these tiny closets are downright dreadful."

"I don't suppose you could donate some of your clothing."

Her eyebrows jumped. "Did you just criticize your client's wardrobe?"

"Not in the least," he assured her. "Your clothing is fabulous. But," and he waved his hand around the closet, "it's a lot of clothing, is all I'm saying." He smirked. "If this isn't enough for one person's clothing…"

Her smile dropped along with his stomach.

"I'm only teasing," he said, reaching out to touch her elbow. "I don't care how much clothing you own."

"I know you're teasing." She offered a brittle smile and he would have sworn a tear glistened. "It's totally fine."

It most definitely was not totally fine. Aaron could see that. But he was unsure what to say next. He'd apologized for his teasing. As snarky as she was, he couldn't have guessed teasing her about her clothes would elicit such a reaction.

Laura returned to the kitchen and he hastened to follow her.

"I'd better put the island back the way we found it," she said.

"I'd have a hard time explaining that to the owner's agent," he agreed.

"We wouldn't want to get you in trouble."

"No, we wouldn't. Or would you?"

Laura grinned, and it appeared that whatever had struck a nerve with her had blown over. "Nah, what fun would that be?"

He returned her grin, glad to see it reappear. She faced the island and held her hands over it, like before. Aaron took a step backward. She hadn't asked for more space, but it still seemed like a good idea to give her room. He realized he could hear her muttering under her breath. He must have missed that the first time.

The area above the butcher block-topped island grew hazy again and slowly regained its earlier shape and appearance. It raised up as wheels materialized. Butcher block faded and became its original stainless steel. The length grew and the island's handles repositioned themselves.

"That is so incredible."

She turned to him, her face flushed with the exertion.

"Are you okay? Did it take more out of you that time?"

Her smile widened and she shook her head, short red hair not budging. "Not at all. This—" She waved her hand in front of her face. "—is from the adrenaline. It's excitement. Although it does require more energy to transform something twice. It's the same reason why I can't transform large amounts of matter."

"Really?"

She pursed her lips in thought. "I'm not completely sure why, to be honest. And, normally, I don't change things back and forth. The changes are permanent."

"How often do you change things?" The entire process fascinated Aaron.

"Not too often."

"How come?"

"I suppose for the same reason that most witches are careful when using their magic." She sat at the staged glass-topped kitchen table and he quickly joined her, their knees almost touching.

"To maintain the energy balance around us?" he asked.

"Yes. I don't know what would happen if I tried too much or too hard, but I'd not want to risk it. You know?"

"Of course," Aaron said. All witches knew that upsetting the natural order was bad.

Her lips turned down again.

"We'll find you the perfect house," he assured her.

"I have no doubt," she agreed. "But maybe we'll pick this up again tomorrow?"

"I have the list of remaining homes we haven't seen, and I'll do a quick check for any new listings in the morning."

Laura abruptly stood and he hastened to follow. "Thank you so much for putting up with me." She bit her lower lip and then offered a weak smile.

"It's not that difficult." He wondered again about her reaction.

"I'll see you in the morning," she called over her shoulder as she sped toward the front door.

"Looking forward to it," he said into the silence that remained. He'd figure out her unexpected emotional shift tomorrow. An intelligent, beautiful, funny woman shouldn't be sad when house-hunting.

CHAPTER THREE

LAURA

What was wrong with me? Laura sat in her Shelby Cobra lookalike, hands gripping the steering wheel, and stared at her rental home beckoning. Not that it beckoned very well. It was a standard beige stucco house with a red-tiled roof. It looked like most of the rest of Wildcrest – and she'd realized in the house-hunting process that she wanted something different. Something that stood out. Something that matched her personality.

With a sigh, she grabbed her leather bag and headed inside, barely registering the house around her. White walls, stark black and white furniture, not a family photo in sight. She lived in a magazine layout. And normally that didn't bother her. She liked the boldness of it. Now, after a month of hanging out with Aaron – no, spending time with him in a professional capacity – she found herself dissatisfied with her beautifully minimalist home. She couldn't identify why that was, only that she'd been feeling off about something.

Laura reached the kitchen and sighed again, though this time laughter bubbled near the surface. Her familiar, Eddie, lay sprawled in the middle of the dark brown kitchen table. Exactly where he wasn't supposed to be. He didn't care, and truth be told, neither did she. It just seemed logical that a cat shouldn't be on a table where people ate.

Eddie opened a single eye, a remarkably human gesture, then stood and stretched, back arched. He yipped at her.

"Edward," she started, and he growled. "You know you're not supposed to be on the table."

The word *Eddie* floated through her mind. That was how they communicated. He sent her images and feelings that her brain translated into visual words. She never fully understood it, and every witch communicated in a distinct style with their familiar, but they'd never had trouble understanding each other.

Now she belly-laughed. He hated being called Edward. His parents called him that back in the nineteenth century. So, of course, she did it when he did something wrong. And he did something wrong by being on the kitchen table.

He leapt from the table, over the ash-colored engineered hardwood floors, and onto the bay window sill. The tabby cat bathed himself while Laura sat at the table and pulled her laptop from the bag.

"I think I freaked out Aaron," she blurted out, and Eddie focused on her. The tears that had been threatening all afternoon spilled over. She was glad for her waterproof mascara.

"What happened?" Eddie asked.

"He thinks I'm an idiot."

"Why?" Disagreement flooded her and she knew that was from Eddie, too.

"I practically burst into tears when we were talking about closet size." She ran her fingers through her slicked back red hair, heedless of ruining the style. Hair stuck out in all directions after.

Eddie jumped back onto the table and padded over to Laura, pushing his nose against her hand. She began petting him, warmth flooding through her.

"Thanks, Eddie." Laura scratched her familiar behind his ears, enjoying the purring that vibrated his little body. The irony was that her great- great- great-uncle, who died in the 1920s, had been a huge, brawny guy, never caught dead without a stylish pin-striped suit. And now he was a six-pound gray-brown tabby cat with uneven whiskers and tufts of hair.

"Why did a closet make you cry? Was it that small?"

Laura chuckled at the questions. "That's what Aaron joked about." She shook her head. "It was his comment about the closet being enough for one person's clothing. One person."

Eddie rolled over on his back so she could scratch his stomach. She obliged him as she talked through what had happened.

"I've always been fine focusing on my career. That was all I had."

Her familiar swiped at her hand. "Hey! What am I, chopped liver?"

"Of course, sorry Eddie," she said. "I've always had you." The purring grew louder. "After my parents died…" She trailed off, thoughts of her parents triggering waves of sadness and guilt. They'd died in a car accident while she'd been away at college. She hadn't been here. Not that she could have done anything. But, still.

As an only child with no living relatives – except Eddie – and a temperament that seemed to push people away, she'd chosen to focus on becoming successful. Plus, she liked computers and IT. The tradeoff seemed worth it, even without having friends or family. One day, she planned to be CEO of Wildcrest Witches International. "I was happy."

Eddie grunted.

"Fine. I was satisfied."

"And now you're not?"

Aaron's smiling face flashed in her mind. "I don't think so."

"What are you going to do?"

"Do?" She made eye contact with her familiar, her face expressing her confusion.

"To become satisfied again."

"Find my new home," she said.

Eddie grunted again.

"What? What's wrong with that?"

"Nothing. If you think that will satisfy you… or make you happy."

"Having my own house to call home will make me happy," she insisted.

"I have no doubt that will help."

"You're thinking me and Aaron?"

"I didn't say that, but since you're thinking it too…"

"No, I don't think so." Her heart fluttered at the statement.

"Why not?"

"He's my real estate agent."

Eddie jumped to his paws and yipped again.

She didn't respond to his yip, which really was the oddest sounding cat noise she'd ever heard.

"So? You can't be friends with your real estate agent."

"Maybe? Yeah, probably."

"Maybe more?"

"What? No!"

"Why not?" Eddie shook his head and returned to the windowsill.

"Because."

"That's not a reason."

Too much baggage, Laura thought. Although more with the Wright family than with him. Of course, if she eliminated every family in town that she had history with, there'd be nobody left.

She wondered if she was making excuses.

CHAPTER FOUR

AARON

"Maybe she's making excuses?" Ben asked before taking a bite of his pastrami sandwich.

His brother's question caught Aaron off-guard. The two sat on high-backed stools at the quartz-topped island in the kitchen of the house they shared with their older brother, Noah. "What do you mean?"

"Maybe she's pretending not to like what you're showing her."

Aaron's face reddened. "You know, I considered showing Laura houses I knew she wouldn't like."

"Don't be like me," Ben warned. The whole family knew about how his ill-planned idea to deliberately mislead his now-girlfriend, Shelly Newsome, had gone wrong. Even if it did end in a happily ever after.

Aaron laughed. "I'm not, I promise. It was a brief, bad idea." He chewed and swallowed a bite of his veggie sandwich. No pastrami for him; when you can communicate with all animals, you stop eating them. "It turned out not to be necessary, anyway. She's very picky. Do you really think she could be pretending? I just thought she was pickier than I'd imagined."

"Do you want her to be pretending?"

"Maybe…" An image of Laura's ruby red smile flickered through his mind and thoughts of her quick wit brought a grin to his face.

"Take your own advice," Ben said, in a not-so-gentle reminder to Aaron of his own strongly worded suggestion when it concerned Ben and Shelly. "Ask her out." Ben stood and brought his plate to the sink. "I've got to get to the hospital. Don't be like me," he repeated with a rueful chuckle.

"I won't," Aaron said, then carried his half-eaten sandwich to his bedroom. There were three bedrooms in the house; one for each of the brothers. Ben's familiar meowed a greeting as Aaron passed the open door. "Hi Cookie." Aaron reached his bedroom door without seeing or hearing his eldest brother's familiar. That wasn't too surprising, since the familiar was a desert rabbit. Maybe Jimmy was burrowed under some of Noah's clothing.

Aaron sat his plate on the wooden nightstand next to his bed and joined his own feline familiar, Elizabeth, on the black bedspread. He flicked the television on and immediately hit mute. He stared around the sparsely decorated room. Aaron wasn't big on *stuff* and preferred an uncluttered space. His small black bookcase included a handful of recent thrillers, but mostly held real estate textbooks from his recently completed degree. No art hung on the walls, though he did have three framed family photographs on his black dresser. One was of him and his two brothers laughing, covered in mud. Somehow his mother caught that shot – they were maybe 10, 11, and 12 in the picture. Another was of his parents, Elijah and Esther Wright.

His father ran their coven and the coven's business, Wildcrest Witches International. His mother, not actually a witch, though whip-smart and empathic, was the Chief Financial Officer. In the photo, the two were radiant, smiling in front of their (at the time) newly completed home. The final photo was of the entire family, probably taken by a friend at a Wiccan celebration. Several of them squinted in the apparent bright sun, so maybe it was summer. He thought it might be Lammas, which was the next big celebration approaching.

"Do you need to talk?" Elizabeth asked, interrupting his reminiscing. The sleek black panther of a house cat was the reincarnation of a great-something-or-other relative from the 1600s. She refused to answer to Liz or Beth; she was Elizabeth, and she was practically royalty.

"Nope," Aaron responded, though kept the television muted and didn't make a move to grab his remaining sandwich.

"I don't believe that's true."

"I talked it out with Ben. I'm good." Now he grabbed his sandwich and took a large bite.

"Uh-huh."

He chewed and swallowed in the awkward silence that followed. "Do you need to talk?" he asked when his mouth was empty.

"Why would I need to talk?" The reproach Aaron heard in the cat's translated meow was crystal clear.

That was the one disadvantage of his magical inclination to be able to communicate with all animals. His already-enhanced ability to communicate with his familiar reached the heights of human communication. And that meant he heard every bit of reproach, sarcasm, or disapproval of Elizabeth. To be fair, he also heard her pure joy, amusement, and gratitude. It was a good trade-off. Most of the time.

Elizabeth sat on her paws in the classic pancake pose of a contented cat and stared at her witch, green eyes wide. "I'm waiting."

Aaron smiled and scratched his familiar behind her ears. She relaxed and began loudly purring. At the continued scratching, her paws soon made gentle biscuits on the bedspread. Love filled him like an overflowing warmth through his body, and he wondered how non-witches experienced their connections with the animals in their care.

"You're not wrong," he finally said, and she rolled over.

"Of course not."

"But I did talk it out with Ben."

"I believe you."

"But I'm still not sure what to do."

"What is the issue?"

"I think I like Laura."

"Yes."

"And I think I want to ask her out."

"And the problem is?"

"I don't know if she'll say yes."

"It's not guaranteed," the cat agreed.

"What if she says no?"

"What if she says yes?"

The echo of a nearly identical conversation with his brother several months ago regarding Ben asking Shelly out rocked Aaron hard. He couldn't be acting just like his brother.

Aaron didn't overthink things. He was the most decisive of the brothers. The most like their force-of-nature father. He never made things harder for himself. Not in his 26 years of being on the planet. Except this time, he was both overthinking and making things harder than they needed to be.

"What are you going to do?" Elizabeth asked.

Time to man up. "I'm going to ask her out."

"When?"

That was an excellent question. "Soon."

The cat chortled and curled up to go to sleep. "You let me know how that goes."

CHAPTER FIVE

LAURA

"The three houses we're seeing this morning just came on the market. Neither will likely last long," Aaron warned Laura.

"Of course," she said, though her focus was on the nearness of Aaron in the small kitchen.

She already knew this wouldn't be the right house. The energy wasn't right. It felt almost physically discordant, like experiencing the sensation of an unattractive paint color, as opposed to only seeing it. But she'd walk around and appear to consider so that Aaron wouldn't think he'd wasted his time.

"How are you doing this morning?" he asked.

"I'm fine." This was the third time he'd asked her how she was doing since she pulled up in front of the house. Her eyes met his – *were those hazel flecks in his green eyes?* – and heat suffused her. "Is there a reason you keep asking me that?" She half-smiled when asking the question.

Aaron took a step back and coughed. "Oh, um, it's just…" He strode to the other side of the small kitchen, which only put a few feet between them. "Yesterday, you seemed upset by my, um, teasing." His face rapidly became the color of a tomato.

Laura suppressed a small laugh. "I promise your teasing didn't upset me." She squashed the discomfort of the reminder that she was alone.

"That's good." He stepped toward her and opened his mouth to continue speaking, but nothing came out.

Anxiety spiked in Laura and she spun around. She didn't understand why she felt anxious. She enjoyed being with Aaron. They were comfortable together, like friends, yet she needed to put space between them. "Let's take a look at the living room. I'd like to see the crown molding."

"Of course," sounded from behind her.

Her heart thumped in her chest and her heels clicked on the stone floor.

"What do you think of this space?" Aaron stood next to her, and she again felt hyper-aware of his presence.

"It's nice."

It really was, to be fair. For a small space, it appeared

bigger, with a wall of windows, white paint, and light-colored stone flooring.

"How are things with my mother?"

Laura arched an eyebrow at the non sequitur. "Fine?"

Aaron chuckled. "You've talked about how much you like working there."

"True enough." She crossed the living room and opened an accordion door around a half-wall, exposing the washer and dryer. *Hmm, that seems like an odd location for the laundry.* "Things are good," Laura answered his question. "Your mother is very easy to get along with."

He grinned. "Most of the time."

"I mean, she is my boss, so there's that."

"In other words, you'd never say anything bad about her to her son."

Laura held her hands up in mock surrender. "Are you trying to get me in trouble?"

"Do you want to get in trouble?"

The double entendre in his question made Laura's stomach drop. She spoke around the sudden cotton balls filling her mouth. "Let's have a look at the closet." She spun on her heels and hurried away from Aaron and his uncomfortable questions. That the questions pleased her but created discomfort was very confusing. He was clearly teasing her, and that was what friends—

She shrieked when a hand touched her shoulder and then spun to face a wide-eyed Aaron.

"Sorry to startle you," he said in a rush.

She gave a shaky laugh. "I have no idea what's wrong with me today." Embarrassment flooded her, and she hoped she didn't look like a fool.

"Let's see the rest of the house."

Laura appreciated that he didn't continue to ask her what was wrong. Especially since she wasn't sure. She was off her game today, that was certain.

Aaron led the way to the master bedroom (*and didn't that also sound like a come-on!*) and she followed, willing her body to quit betraying her with these weird overreactions.

"This is a lovely room," she said, as she looked around. "I like the tray ceiling." Both of them gazed upward. The tray ceiling added a three-dimensional effect and helped the smallish room seem larger. "It wouldn't be a requirement, but could be a nice extra."

"I'll add that to the nice-to-have list."

"Although my lists are eliminating most of the homes we're seeing."

"They are. That's okay. It just means we haven't found the right one."

"Of course."

"It's the law of averages."

"It is?"

"We live in a small town where not many people leave." He shrugged. "When there aren't a ton of options, most of them probably won't work. Or something like that."

"In other words, I'm never finding a new home." She didn't mean that the way it came out, and laughed.

"Yes, you are."

"Yes, I am. Eventually," she said. "You may be stuck with me for a while."

"That wouldn't be so bad."

"No?"

"No." He lifted a hand as if to touch her and then dropped it. "Let's look at the master bathroom."

"Lead the way," she said before following behind him, enjoying the view. The man wore a suit well, that was clear.

The small bathroom matched the rest of the house. It was all lovely. However, like she'd suspected, the energy didn't work for her. She hoped the next house would be a better fit. Although the thought of the house hunting with Aaron ending led to a swelling of sadness. She didn't want it to end, if she was being honest with herself.

Maybe Eddie was right. Maybe she should ask him out. At that thought, a frisson of anxiety rose again. Something was telling her not to get involved with him. Some part of her didn't think it was a good idea. He was intelligent, sweet, and funny – and hot, truth be told – but he wasn't a good fit for her. She worked for his mother. There was that complication, among others.

Or was she making excuses?

"Earth to Laura."

Aaron's voice jolted Laura out of her ruminations and

she offered a half-smile. "Sorry about that. I was thinking about the next house."

"Ah, so we've eliminated this one, then?"

"I would say so."

He made an elaborate show of pressing delete on his phone. She supposed he was deleting a saved listing sheet and chuckled.

"That was dramatic," she said.

"I try to be entertaining."

"Well done, then."

"Shall we go to the next house?"

"Lead the way, Aaron."

CHAPTER SIX

AARON

Aaron didn't understand why this was so awkward. Ever since he teased her yesterday, their easy conversation seemed stilted and forced. She kept saying everything was fine, though it seemed clear it wasn't. Unless he was reading into things now. He knew he hadn't yesterday, but today was a new day.

He parked his black Jeep Cherokee in front of the next house and watched Laura pull in behind him in her little sports car. She looked radiant as always, this time in black slacks and a purple V-neck wrap shirt. He loved how she kept her short red hair off her face, accenting her flawless skin and sparkling eyes.

Ugh. This had to be a crush. His familiar was right. He needed to ask her out.

But, first, time to work.

Aaron joined Laura at the start of the walkway leading to the house's front door. "First impressions?"

Laura's lips thinned into a line. Not of displeasure. Of deep thought. When she was thinking about something, she really thought about it.

He waited while her gaze flicked around the exterior of the house. It was the typical beige stucco that the vast majority of the homes had, which he knew wasn't her preference. But it also had several large windows, suggesting plentiful natural light inside. Plus, a wide porch ran half the length of the house.

"This is nice," she said, nodding. "It has potential."

"Let's have a look inside."

Aaron followed Laura to the door, watching her eyes taking in everything from the paver pathway and porch to the teal front double doors. When she caught her breath after they walked inside, he had a good feeling about this one.

"What do you think?" he asked.

"This is very nice," she said.

Aaron tried to view the house through her very picky eyes. The open floor plan showcased the vaulted ceilings and dark, wide-beam wood flooring. After entering, a short hallway to the left led to the garage and a guest suite.

Another guest bedroom and a small den were to the right. Further into the house was a grand chef's kitchen and dining area, which led into the living room.

"Look at that view," she gushed. Sliding glass doors at the back of the house showcased an amazing view of the desert and nearby low mountains. "I didn't realize this was right on the edge of town. I don't know how I missed that."

"We've seen a lot of houses."

"Fair enough."

They stood together, gazing out the back of the house at the green of the desert shrubs, contrasting with the brown rocks and red of the distant mountains. It truly was a beautiful view.

"This may be the one," she whispered.

At her words, Aaron's heart stopped. But she didn't mean him. She meant the house.

"The energy is right," she continued, more to herself than to him.

"Do you want to see the rest of the home first?"

Laura turned and unexpectedly hugged him. "Yes, I do. Thank you for finding this."

The feel of her arms around him and the light scent of vanilla lotion tickling his nostrils flooded him with joy. And left him feeling bereft when she withdrew.

Her smile lit up her face.

"Let's look at the rest," he said.

Aaron led her through the other two bedrooms and

bathrooms, then out to the back porch, where she debated herself on whether she needed to screen the porch. She ultimately decided it wasn't necessary. He agreed with her assessment. The smile never left her face the entire time she explored. Unlike in the other houses, she peeked into every nook and cranny this time, clearly indicating this house was different. He'd be shocked if she didn't submit an offer. And while he was thrilled for her, his disappointment at the idea of not seeing her regularly once she bought the home bothered him.

He couldn't account for the awkwardness he'd felt in their conversation. But she said it was okay. And it was going well in this house. Plus, both his brother and his familiar said to go for it.

It wasn't like him to be this wishy-washy. He went for whatever he wanted. And he knew he wanted Laura.

Time to man up.

They'd found their way back to the kitchen. Laura was opening and closing the multiple white cabinets, mumbling about where she would put things.

She'd obviously decided this was the one and she would make it happen. His mother had told him what a go-getter Laura was. That was one thing he liked about her, too. She was like him. Decisive. Well, most of the time.

Aaron stood next to her at the perfectly sized butcher block-topped island with a smile. "Seems like this is the one."

Her eyes shone. "Yes. 100%. Everything about it is perfect. Even the energy feels right." She ran her hand along the top of the island and sighed with apparent happiness.

"I'm so glad we found the one. I'll pull the comps and we can discuss the offer you want to make."

"Perfect. Can we do that today? I don't want to miss out."

"Absolutely. You won't miss out. I'll let the listing agent know we'll be submitting an offer. I can also check if they've received any other recent offers."

Her face clouded at his words. "I'm not losing this house."

He put a hand on her arm. "You won't. I won't let that happen." The words came out before he could stop them. That wasn't a promise he could make, but it was worth it for the blinding smile she offered in return.

"Thank you so much, Aaron. For everything." Her eyes were dilated and if he wasn't mistaken, her voice had taken on a husky tone.

"Would you like to go to dinner with me?" He blurted the question and, at her reaction, wanted to take the invitation back.

She stumbled back a step away from him, her mouth forming a perfect, gorgeous ruby red circle of surprise.

"No."

CHAPTER SEVEN

LAURA

Laura's brain emptied at the unexpected question. Although, if she was honest, it wasn't that unexpected. He obviously felt the same pull she did. But, if that was the case, she had to wonder about her instant negative reaction. Oh, wait, he was apologizing.

"—if I've overstepped. That wasn't my intention. I thought…" he trailed off.

She offered a half-shrug. "There's no reason to apologize. I just don't think we're a good fit." She knew that made no sense, but that was all she had.

Aaron gave a sharp nod.

"I work for your mother and we're business associates."

At that, he cocked an eyebrow. "What?"

"Should you date clients?"

"I'd think that's my choice. Plus, we just found you the perfect house."

Laura's face flushed. She couldn't believe this was the explanation she was giving. There was no way she'd accept that excuse from him if he'd said it. It wasn't like they worked together in an office.

"If I ask you out again in a month after we close, will you say yes then?" His smirk confirmed he was teasing, though it pointed out the ridiculousness of her excuse.

"I'll still be working for your mother after we close, but ask me out again then and we'll see," she said in response, surprising even herself with her flirtatious tone. Her prior crush on his brother would still be in their shared past in a month. It seemed weird to go out with the brother of someone she'd crushed on. And yet, she'd put it out there anyway. Because maybe this was just another excuse.

"I will." His eyes dilated as he promised.

Laura swallowed hard and reached out to touch his arm. "Thank you for understanding."

He covered her hand with his. "Always."

There seemed to be subtext here, and she didn't know what it was. "You said there was a third house?"

He appeared more confused by her question itself than the fact that it was an abrupt non sequitur. "I thought you were submitting an offer on this house?"

"I am. Just trying to be thorough. Maybe the next house will be perfect."

"More perfect than this one?"

Laura groaned inwardly that her attempt to avoid the discomfort by focusing on the house hunting was failing. "We won't know unless we check," she answered his question while striding toward the door. And swore she heard chuckling as he hurried to follow her.

"I'll text you the address."

"Thank you," she called out over her shoulder, avoiding eye contact, before hiding in her car and watching him enter his Jeep and then fiddle with his phone. She wanted to grab herself by the shoulders and give herself a hard shake.

She was acting like a teenager. So what, he asked her out and she said no? It wasn't the end of the world and they could still work together.

Her car roared to life and she plugged the address he'd texted into the navigation app, although she had a general idea of its location. The town wasn't big enough for there to be streets she wasn't familiar with.

Her mind refused to stop swirling over and around her one-word answer to his question.

No.

She wanted to say yes. But she also needed to say no.

There was too much baggage. Between her and his family. Between her and her past.

Or maybe it was all in her head.

Despite beating herself up during the five-minute drive to the new house for how she handled his question, she was composed when she joined him on the sidewalk.

"First impressions?"

"Meh."

"That good, huh?"

She echoed his chuckle. "It doesn't match my energy," she said with a shrug, but he nodded. As a witch, she figured he understood that you never underestimate the power of matching energy. "Since we're here, though, let's go ahead and take a look."

"To be thorough," he said, using her phrase.

"To be thorough."

Aaron stopped short right before reaching the porch, causing Laura to nearly crash into him.

"What is it?" she asked.

He frowned and swiveled his head. "I'm hearing someone."

Laura cocked her head. "I don't hear anything. What does it sound like?"

"It's hard to explain. Like someone mumbling."

"How would you hear that?" she asked out of curiosity and not disbelief.

"That's why it's hard to explain," he said before squinting in concentration. "It's almost like—" he cut off midsentence.

"Aaron?" She was worried now that maybe he was hearing voices that weren't there.

"Don't worry, they're real," he said, as if reading her thoughts. He walked to the side of the stucco house, crossing the artificial turf lawn. He broke into a trot after he rounded the corner. "Hey there."

"Oh!" Laura exclaimed. A small reddish-hued cocker spaniel sat curled against the side of the house. "What did you hear? Was the dog barking? How could I have missed a dog barking?"

Aaron waggled his eyebrows. "Not exactly." He approached the dog, who stood and wagged its tail. "What's your name?"

This time the dog barked.

"It's nice to meet you, Ginger. I'm Aaron and this is Laura."

Laura waved uncertainly at the dog. Ginger, she corrected herself. The dog had a name. That she had told Aaron. Laura was enthralled watching Aaron speak with Ginger. An animal that wasn't a familiar. So cool.

"What are you doing here? This house is for sale." Aaron frowned while Ginger limped around, alternating between silently staring and barking at him. "Slow down. I'm not getting all of that."

"Is Ginger okay?"

"No, but I'm having a hard time teasing apart what she's saying. She's very excitable," he said.

Laura could see that. Ginger continued to move around, barking over and over. "I have an idea." Laura stood tall and cleared her throat. "Sit, Ginger." The dog stopped moving though didn't obey. "Sit, Ginger," Laura repeated. The dog's rump hit the turf. "Good girl." Laura scratched the top of Ginger's head as a reward and turned to Aaron with a grin. "She and I don't understand each other, so there's no need for her to get excited trying to tell me anything. But I hoped she was trained and would recognize the word, sit."

"Sometimes simpler is better," Aaron agreed, matching Laura's grin.

"Now try to find out what's going on with Ginger."

Aaron dropped to Ginger's level and maintained eye contact. "Tell me what we need to know, Ginger. How can we help?"

CHAPTER EIGHT

AARON

Communicating with animals comprised an interesting mix of images and words appearing in Aaron's mind. Not that the animals knew English, of course. It was more that his magical inclination acted like a universal translator for a lot of what they communicated. Not everything, though. And, in those cases, images could flood his mind from the animal trying to convey a message.

Like in this instance.

The senior pup had indeed flooded Aaron's mind, to the point that it made him dizzy. Luckily, Laura's brilliant approach calmed the excited dog and now she waited for the next instructions.

Ginger stared at Aaron, sad whines escaping her throat. Her almond-shaped brown eyes begged him for help.

"Okay, Ginger. How can we help?" Aaron repeated his question.

A face appeared in Aaron's mind. Slight lines around dark brown eyes in a tanned face. Shaggy black hair carelessly brushed off his face. A friendly face. "Who is this, Ginger?"

The cocker spaniel lifted a paw, almost like she was going to shake hands, but then shook her head instead, in a very human gesture.

Instead of an answer, a new face appeared in Aaron's mind. Thinner brown hair framed brown eyes in a more wrinkled face. This face appeared friendly, too, and possibly related to the first image. "Who are these men, Ginger? Is one of them your owner? Do you live here?"

Ginger barked, "Yes."

Aaron realized his mistake. Three questions in a row and a single answer. "Sorry about that, Ginger. Let's take one at a time. Do you live here?" He hoped not, since the house was unoccupied and for sale.

Instead of answering Aaron's question, another whine escaped Ginger's throat. She dropped from sitting to laying on the ground and began panting.

Aaron placed his hands gently on either side of the dog's face, the dog's actions reminding him of the prior limping. "Are you hurt? Where does it hurt?" He realized his error of asking multiple questions again. Ginger whinnied before he could clarify.

"Leg."

"Which leg?" Aaron rocked back on his heels to better view her legs. One of her back legs appeared angled wrong. That fit with the limping they'd seen. "Anything else?"

"Inside," Ginger barked. She rested her head on the artificial turf. Her eyes never left his.

"I don't know what she said, but that high pitch doesn't sound good," Laura whispered from behind Aaron and Ginger.

Aaron had almost forgotten Laura was there. He looked up at her. "No, it doesn't. Let me call my brother."

Laura bit her lower lip while Aaron called Ben, though all she said was, "Okay."

"Ben?" Aaron asked, his hand not holding the phone continuing to stroke Ginger's fur.

Hey little brother sounded in Aaron's ear.

"Laura and I—" Aaron ignored Ben's chuckle into the phone. "—found a hurt dog while house hunting. Can I bring her to you?"

Of course, Ben agreed, all business. *I'm with Mom at the company.*

"We'll be right there. See you soon," Aaron said, and disconnected. "Ben's at Wildcrest Witches International. We're going to bring Ginger there."

If Laura wondered why they were heading to her place

of employment on a weekend to see Ben instead of a veterinarian, she didn't say anything.

"I'm going to pick you up now," Aaron said to Ginger before wrapping the dog in his strong arms and lifting her. He turned to Laura. "Will we fit in your car or can you drive my Jeep?"

"It's probably better to take the Jeep," Laura said after a moment's consideration.

Together they walked to the vehicle and got situated. While Laura drove, careful of any bumps in the road that might hurt the injured Ginger, Aaron continued to speak with the senior in his lap.

"I know it hurts. Can you tell me anything more? Do you know the names of the men you showed me?"

Laura's brow furrowed at his questions, though Aaron didn't answer her unspoken ones. He'd explain when he explained to Ben.

Images of the men, a blue nondescript sedan, and a blacktop road swirled in Aaron's mind. But only one word. "Help."

"Don't worry, Ginger. We're going to help you. And we'll do what we can to help you find your owner." The sweet girl liked that and wagged her tail at Aaron, who scratched her ears and under her chin. Aaron met Laura's concerned eyes. "Ginger's confused, maybe from the pain, and so what I'm getting isn't clear. But, either way, we need to find her owner."

CHAPTER NINE

LAURA

The drive to Wildcrest Witches International passed quickly and soon Laura was parking the Jeep in a spot outside the one-story stucco building that almost resembled a ranch-style home. The coven's company wasn't big, so they didn't need much space. Aaron exited the vehicle, careful not to jostle Ginger. Laura moved ahead to open the front door for them. She used her key card to open the doors and held one open for Aaron to bring the ailing dog through.

"Thanks." Aaron walked through the foyer, straight for the glass double doors that led to the back row of offices. He hooked a left, presumably toward his mother's office.

Aaron hadn't explained why they had taken Ginger to his brother, instead of a veterinarian. When they entered his mother's office and she saw Ben standing beside the empty walnut desk, it hit her. Ben's magical inclination was to know what someone needed when they were sick. She hadn't realized that extended from humans to animals. It made sense; humans were animals, too.

"Mom stepped out but will be right back. Bring the dog to me," Ben instructed his brother. "Hey Laura. Nice to see you."

Laura nodded in greeting, unable to speak. Ben. Her high school crush. Currently dating her high school frenemy Shelly Newsome. He looked great as always, but that was all. She didn't feel the emotions she'd felt years ago. And that made sense. The crush had been years earlier. She didn't still have feelings for him.

So why should that get in the way of seeing Aaron?

The question snuck in and before she could explore it, she refocused her attention on the brothers discussing Ginger.

"Hey sweetheart, I know it hurts," Ben said. He ran his fingers through Ginger's fur, causing her to wriggle her butt. After manipulating her limbs a little and hovering his hands over sections of her body, especially her leg and chest, Ben patted her head a final time.

"What's the word?" Aaron asked.

"Her leg might be broken and a couple of ribs are maybe

bruised. There doesn't seem to be any organ damage. The damage is consistent with blunt force trauma."

"Someone hit her," Laura exclaimed, a hand fluttering to cover her mouth.

Ben nodded. "Or she hit something."

"Like hit by a car?" Aaron asked. When Ben nodded, Aaron directed his next question to Ginger. "What happened?"

Laura watched Aaron, fascinated, as he nodded in response to a series of yips from Ginger. After a few exchanges, Aaron addressed Ben and Laura.

"She keeps showing me a picture of a car, but I can't nail it down more than that. The car and the pictures of two similar-looking men. One of these men could be the owner. Or could be the one who threw her from a car, or hit her with a car. I really can't be more precise."

"That's okay," Laura said, laying a hand on his forearm, not missing the sly smile on Ben's face at the movement. She ignored Aaron's brother. "This gives us a great place to start."

"In the meantime, I'm heading back to the hospital and can drop Ginger at the vet on my way," Ben offered.

"Thanks," Aaron said.

"Perfect. That will give us a chance to do some sleuthing into the men Ginger keeps showing you, Aaron," Laura said.

"What do you suggest?"

"We can use my computer to cross-reference property records with social media—" she answered.

"I can check with the listing agent as well," Aaron added.

"—and between these, we might be able to identify the men and confirm if one of them is the owner."

"Also, if one of them hurt her," Aaron said darkly. He scratched Ginger behind the ears, then carefully ran his hand over the length of her body.

"Hopefully, there's a simpler explanation." Laura refused to believe someone would deliberately hurt Ginger.

"There may be," Ben concurred. "It could have been an accident. Blunt force trauma doesn't have to be an attack or purposeful violence."

A wide smile lit up Aaron's face. "You're both right. I can't imagine someone in Wildcrest doing something harmful like that."

"Exactly," Laura said. The supernatural beings in Wildcrest cared for nature more than most. That didn't mean there couldn't be a sinister witch, but the chances were much lower in their small town.

"I was hoping to see Mom before I left," Ben said, glancing toward the open office door. "But I'm not sure how long her meeting is going to last."

"If it's with someone from book club, it could be another hour," Aaron joked.

Laura joined the brothers in chuckling. Even she knew

about Esther's reading addiction. She loved books and read several every week. At least once a week, Laura popped into Esther's office, only to see her engrossed in a book. 'Just one more chapter' was practically a mantra for Esther.

"We'll let her know you still needed to talk to her," Aaron offered.

"Thanks," Ben said, and leaned over to pick up Ginger from his mother's desk.

A voice from the door interrupted the conversation. "Aaron! So great to see you. Laura, how did the house hunting go?"

Laura turned at the sound of her boss's voice. "Hi Esther. It went well. I think we found the winner."

"That's wonderful." Esther entered her office and then startled when she saw a dog on her desk. "Whose dog is that? She's adorable."

Aaron brought Esther up to speed.

"Oh, Ben, that's wonderful that you can bring Ginger to the vet so Aaron and Laura can go on their lunch date."

"Date?" Laura asked. She and Aaron wore matching expressions of surprise, and Ben tried unsuccessfully to hide a smirk.

"Well, yes." Esther's brow furrowed. "I thought you were going to lunch after looking at houses. Isn't that what you said, Aaron?"

CHAPTER TEN

AARON

"Um," Aaron eloquently responded as his mother crossed her office to her desk. "I didn't say it was a date." When he saw Laura's flushed face, his heart sank. He never should have told his mother that he was asking Laura out. She'd asked him how the house hunting was going, and he'd slipped and confessed.

"Hmm." Esther sat behind her desk and crossed her long legs. "I could have sworn you said it was a date. But perhaps I misunderstood."

"Yeah, Mom, I'm sorry, you did misunderstand," Aaron said in a rush. "I definitely didn't say it was a date. We're work colleagues." His voice stuttered on the last sentence.

Ben and Esther both lifted eyebrows in matching expressions of disbelief. "Work colleagues?" his mother asked.

"Yes. I'm her realtor," he answered, as if that made any sense.

"Sure, of course," Esther said and folded her hands on the desktop.

Aaron wished a hole would open up below him and swallow him whole. That would be preferable to the excruciating embarrassment of having his mother tell the woman he was interested in that he'd talked to her about that interest.

He wondered if Laura could use her ability to manipulate matter to open that hole beneath him. She'd said she could only manipulate small amounts of matter, but she also said she'd changed pieces of an entire car. Perhaps creating a hole in the floor would be easy. Of course, then there was the matter of where he'd go. There was no basement in the building, so she might need to change more matter, perhaps manipulate the concrete base of the building.

Aaron knew that his frenzied thoughts were an obvious effort to avoid remaining in this conversation, or thinking about what his mother said to Laura.

Laura. She was flushed so red she looked like she was having a heart attack or something. No doubt she'd love to make him vanish, too.

Ben chuckled and stood, cradling Ginger to his chest. "On that supremely awkward note," he said with a snort. "I'll take sweet Ginger to the vet."

"Let us know how she's doing," Aaron requested, thrilled with the topic change. He stopped his brother from walking past and scratched Ginger's head. "You're going to be okay. My brother will take good care of you."

Ginger barked. "Feel better."

"Yes, you're going to feel much better," he assured her.

She barked again, and the images of the two men flittered through his mind.

"We'll figure out who those two are," he promised. He held his hand in front of her face and she licked him, then gave a happy sigh.

"Okay, that's enough of that," Ben said. "Let me get her to the vet."

Aaron stepped aside and he, Laura, and Esther watched Ben leave with the cocker spaniel cradled in his arms.

Silence descended on the room. The three stared at each other. Aaron cleared his throat. "How was your meeting, Mom?"

Esther seemed a bit put out by the question and didn't answer.

Aaron wondered if that meant the meeting didn't go well.

"The meeting was fine. Everything is set for the next release," she said.

Laura nodded at the statement. Aaron was confused. He was on the Board of Directors of Wildcrest Witches International, though he rarely interacted unless they needed him for something specific. Whatever the release was, it didn't concern him, apparently.

"Is everything okay, Esther?" Laura asked, approaching the desk.

So, it wasn't just him that noticed his mother seemed… irritated wasn't the right word, but it was close.

His mother closed her brown eyes, then fanned herself with a rolled-up piece of paper. "I'm fine." She set the paper down and frowned. "I don't know."

"Mom? Should I call Ben back to check on you?" If something was wrong with their mother, Ben would be able to tell.

"What?" She appeared startled by that suggestion. "No, that's unnecessary. I got hot for a moment." She stood from the desk. "But maybe I'll head home."

Laura placed a hand on Esther's elbow. "That might not be a bad idea. And since it's the weekend, and you're the CFO, I don't think anyone's going to give you a hard time," she joked.

Esther smiled wanly. "True enough."

Aaron closely watched his mother walk to the office door. Per usual, she looked sharp in a business suit, with her long brown hair held back in a loose bun. Esther appeared fine, steady on her feet and with no evidence of confusion. Maybe she was coming down with something. He frowned. He'd call his brother later anyway, to check in with him about it.

"Have a good lunch that isn't a date," Esther said from the doorway.

Aaron winced at the comment, uncertain whether he was reading a tone in it. Surely not. After all, he couldn't think of a reason his mother would be unhappy that he wasn't going out on a date with Laura. She supported whatever Aaron did; she wasn't an overbearing mother.

"Enjoy your half-day," Laura said before Esther disappeared out of the office.

They listened to his mother's heels on the tile floor until they faded away, and then stared at each other.

"I'm sorry about that. I'm not sure where she got that from," Aaron said lamely, wondering why he didn't just tell her the truth. He was blunt with everyone else.

Laura's cheeks tinted pink again and she waved away his apology and pathetic lack of explanation. "No worries," she assured him. "You did ask me out, so maybe you did say something to her about planning that."

"Yeah, that's true," he admitted, wishing again for that hole to open up. He didn't know why this bothered him so much. He'd asked other women out who had said no. It wasn't that big of a deal. Except this time, it was.

"But we have work to do. We need to find Ginger's owner."

"What should we do first?" Aaron asked, thankful for the distraction and the opportunity to help the cocker spaniel.

"Let's head to my office and start researching. We can order food."

CHAPTER ELEVEN

LAURA

The walk to Laura's room took but a minute, though felt much longer. The awkwardness in Esther Wright's office reverberated around them as they crossed the building from there to Laura's.

"Are you ready to find Ginger's owner?" Laura asked, taking a seat at her walnut desk. All the executive offices contained the same furniture. No particular reason for that, she assumed, other than expediency. Artwork and knickknacks provided touches of personality and color. In her case, photographs of the surrounding mountains covered her walls.

"Is that one new?" Aaron asked instead, peering at a

vivid image of snow-capped mountain peaks.

"Yes," she answered, joining him before the latest image. "I took that this past winter."

"It's gorgeous."

"Thank you. It doesn't do it justice." Laura was keenly aware of how close they stood to each other while admiring her handiwork. She cleared her throat and moved away from his heat to sit again behind her desk. "What do you want me to order for lunch? I can see if *Magic Eats* doesn't have a wait."

"Perfect. I'll take a grilled cheese sandwich with fries."

Laura checked online. The 1950s-style diner was popular in town, but it looked like they weren't busy today. That was a lucky break. She stuck with a veggie sandwich for herself; Aaron was a vegetarian, and even though she knew he didn't mind if those around him ate meat, she chose not to.

She finished the order and smiled at Aaron. "You ready?"

"Yes, ma'am," he joked with a salute, then took the brown leather chair opposite her and whipped out his cellphone. "I'll call the listing agent on the house where we found Ginger and get the name of the owner."

Laura was already clicking keys on her keyboard. "I'll check the county for the official property owner to confirm." She clicked through to the property assessor's website, and with a few more clicks, entered the address in the search bar for the records.

Meanwhile, Aaron located the listing agent's number and called her. "Hi Lisa, it's Aaron."

Laura tuned his conversation out while scrolling to the exact address of the home. She jotted down the name listed for the property owner just as Aaron concluded his call.

"Jack Panner?" she asked.

"Jack Panner," he confirmed.

"Did you get a phone number for Mr. Panner?"

"I did."

"Let's give Mr. Panner a call and find out if he's Ginger's owner." Excitement rose in Laura that they might solve their mystery so quickly.

Aaron typed the number into his cellphone, then held it up to his ear. After a moment, he gave a quick shake of his head. "Voicemail," he told her, then, "Good afternoon Mr. Panner. This is Aaron Wright. I'm a real estate agent. Your agent Lisa gave me your number. If you could, please call me when you have a chance." Aaron ended the message with his phone number.

"Now we wait," he said.

"Not quite," Laura disagreed. She began typing again, talking to him as she did. "Now that we have a name, we can look him up on social media to see if his picture matches what Ginger showed you." She scrolled through profile names. "Okay, there are several Jack Panners, but only one here in Wildcrest. If he's kept his location updated, this could be him!" She waved Aaron over. "Do you want to see his picture?"

Aaron came around the desk to stand beside Laura in her chair. He leaned over to look at the photograph. It was of a man hiking in the desert. "Can you make it bigger?"

"Yep," she answered, double-clicking on the picture. Aaron's light musk wafted over her and she barely stopped herself from inhaling deeply. That would have been awkward. When his arm bumped hers, the physical contact gave her goosebumps.

"That's him," he said. "That's one of the images Ginger showed me. He has to be her owner."

Laura stood and impulsively threw her arms around Aaron. He stiffened a moment and then they melded together, warmth flowing over them as they reveled in their success and enjoyed the closeness. Although she wondered about the fact that she'd now hugged him twice in one day. That was most definitely not like her. At all. And yet.

"Good job," Aaron whispered.

"You too."

Aaron's cellphone rang, and he released Laura before pulling the phone from his pocket. "It's him," he said before answering. "Hello, this is Aaron Wright." He listened to a voice on the other end, his smile growing wider. "Yes, I'm calling about your house for sale, but not for the reason you're probably thinking." Aaron explained about finding Ginger and asked if he was her owner.

When Aaron's smile fell, Laura flattened her palms against the desk and bit her lower lip. That didn't look good.

"Do you know anybody who may have lost a cocker spaniel? Her name is Ginger." He listened to the response. "No? That's too bad. If you think—"

Aaron stopped mid-sentence and Laura perked up. "Does he have an idea?" she whispered.

"Okay, thank you," Aaron said. "That's a great help." He ended the call and retook his seat. "Give me a sec to type out some names."

"Of course," Laura said, but he was already typing. Her phone dinged. "The food is here. I'll go grab it."

She hurried through the house and collected the meals from Billy the delivery driver. When she returned to her office, Aaron had finished and was waiting to explain what he'd learned. She spread out the food and they ate while they talked.

"Jack said he'd listed his house *For Sale by Owner* for a day or so before giving the listing to an agent yesterday, since he unexpectedly would be heading out of town for a couple of weeks. He says he remembered showing the house to a guy who had a cocker spaniel. He couldn't be sure which guy it was, so he gave me three names of people he showed the house to before he decided to go with a realtor."

"Give me the names," Laura said and he slid his

cellphone across the desk. She typed the first into the search bar.

"Do you have a picture for me to see?"

Laura shook her head while she answered, "There's a picture, but this guy is bald, so I doubt he's the other one Ginger showed you."

"Ah, okay. Try lucky number two."

"Hmm, this one is a maybe. Let me open another browser window and get a picture of the third man, and then you can compare them." A few more keystrokes and she spun the laptop around to face him. "Um, no need for you to get up again."

"Sure," he said, though she thought she saw disappointment flare.

Because he wouldn't be able to stand near her again? Or maybe that was wishful thinking on her part.

He focused on the photographs blown up on the screen. "This one," he crowed, pointing. "Definitely this one. The one on the left," he clarified as she turned the laptop back toward herself.

"Marvin Kelm," Laura read from the screen. "Hmm." She frowned. "He hasn't posted anything in days."

"Maybe he's not active on social media?"

She scrolled further down the page. "No, before that, he posted every day. Including pictures of Ginger!"

Aaron held up his hands and they shared a congratulatory high-five.

"Now we need to find him." Laura typed some more. "I've got a number." She entered the number and mouthed *voicemail* when Marvin Kelm's voicemail greeting started. "Good afternoon, Mr. Kelm. My name is Laura Harkin and I believe my… friend… and I found your dog, Ginger. Please call me at your earliest convenience. We'd love to return her to you." She concluded the call and frowned at Aaron.

"What's wrong? Ginger's being treated right now anyway, so it's not a big deal that we didn't reach him right away."

"I know, but what if something happened to him? To Marvin Kelm?" She nibbled her lower lip. "I know it's only social media, but he hasn't posted anything. Not even looking for his lost dog."

Now Aaron's frown matched hers. "Do you think he's been hurt? Or worse?"

Laura's eyes widened. "I hope not. Maybe you can check with your brother to see if he's been admitted to the hospital."

"That's a great idea. I'll text him the name and picture, and ask."

Laura watched Aaron while he did just that, admiring his strong jaw and how he stuck his tongue out like his brother did when he was thinking. Must be a family trait.

Aaron looked up and caught her staring. She flushed and he waggled his eyebrows. "Like what you see?"

Her mouth dropped open at the flirtation, and she changed the subject. "Should we head to the hospital now? Just in case?"

He seemed to smother a smile at her not-very-smooth topic change. "Sure, why not? Maybe Ben will have an answer for us by the time we arrive."

CHAPTER TWELVE

AARON

"After we reunite Ginger with her owner, I have a couple more homes to show you," Aaron said as they sat in his Jeep at the one stoplight between Wildcrest Witches International and Wildcrest Hospital.

Laura laughed. "Oh, no, I'm finished. I'm ready to put in an offer on the house from earlier. The one before the one where we found the dog."

He'd remembered she'd said that, but secretly hoped she wasn't ready. Although, her other words came back to him, too. "Ah, because once you buy the house, I can ask you out." His eyes cut to her as he accelerated through the intersection.

"Oh. Right. I said that, didn't I?"

"You did." His heart pounded while he waited for the next sentence to come out of her mouth. He didn't have to wait long.

"I guess we'll see what happens," she said in a playful tone.

He didn't have a snappy comeback for that, and the silence stretched for the final few minutes of the drive. After he parked and turned off the car, Aaron faced her.

"Wait," he said, reaching for her arm before she could open her door.

"Yes?"

Aaron didn't speak. He opened his mouth, closed it. "I'm glad we're on this adventure together," he finally said.

"Me too." Her hand reached across the center console.

He held his breath. Her fingers grazed his cheek. They leaned toward each other. And just when Aaron thought their lips would meet, she jerked backward.

"We should finish this adventure," she said, the unspoken *first* floating between them.

"Okay," he whispered.

Aaron barely noticed crossing the parking lot. She almost kissed him. Or he almost kissed her. Whichever it was, he felt phantom lips on his. An arriving text brought him back to the moment.

Laura looked at him. "Ben?"

"Yep." He scanned the text. "Nobody by that name, but

there is a John Doe who resembles the photo. He gave me a room number to meet him in, in about ten minutes."

"Okay, sounds good," Laura said, and then tripped over a pothole near the sidewalk.

Aaron caught her by the arm and pulled him to her to prevent her fall. "Are you okay?"

She breathed into his ear – she was so tall! – and shakily replied yes.

"They really should fix that," he mumbled, more to himself than to Laura.

"I can," she said, and stood over the break in the blacktop.

"You what?"

"I can fix it."

"You can fix—" he started, then stopped. "Right, of course." He stepped back to watch the literal magic.

Laura concentrated on the hole and, like when she'd manipulated the kitchen island at the house for sale, the area above the hole grew hazy. It darkened and the blacktop appeared to move of its own volition.

Aaron bit back a snort. The movement reminded him of the movie *The Blob*.

"Wait." Laura frowned. A bead of sweat broke out on her forehead.

As Aaron watched, the center of the new blacktop crumbled and collapsed in on itself, leaving the hole bigger than it was before.

"I don't understand." She concentrated harder. The haze reappeared and the process repeated.

Including the part where it fell apart. Now the hole was twice the size it had been before Laura attempted her magic.

"I don't understand," she repeated.

Before she could try a third time, Aaron stopped her. "I don't know what's happening either, but maybe we should just let the hospital know they have a pothole that could cause an accident." He said the words gently, and still her eyes shined with tears when she looked at him.

"That's never happened before."

"Let's check in with Ben. Maybe he can see if there's something on the fritz with you." His attempt at a jovial tone worked and she cracked a slight smile.

"Maybe I'm tired," she said. "But I'll let Ben look me over, anyway."

CHAPTER THIRTEEN

LAURA

I'll let Ben look me over. Laura couldn't believe how that sounded, but Aaron didn't react, so maybe it was all in her head.

"Let's find the room Ben texted," Aaron said after they entered the hospital's sliding glass doors. He beelined for the elevator.

Laura was slower to follow, her mind stuck on her magic not working.

"You coming?" He held the door open with one arm and beckoned her with the other.

"Yes, sorry." She stepped into the elevator and stood beside him, very aware of his closeness. "I was thinking."

Aaron touched her hand. "It's going to be okay."

Of course, he knew what she'd been thinking about. A witch without magic. Well, that was like missing a part of yourself.

The elevator doors opened and Laura snickered. Tall Ben towered over short Shelly where they stood outside a room at the far end of the hall. Not that long ago, Shelly had had an issue with not feeling like a witch, because of her own misfiring magic. Laura now had a small sense of her former frenemy's frustration.

Ben and Shelly waved as Laura and Aaron approached.

Before she could lose her nerve from the risk of embarrassment, Laura blurted out her request. "Ben, I'd rather not discuss the specifics, but can you tell me if anything seems off? Anything medically?"

Although Ben quirked an eyebrow, he didn't question. "Of course." He eyed her up and down, in a clinical way, though she still felt her throat tighten.

Thankfully, it didn't appear that he needed to go hands-on with checking. Laura thought she'd have a stroke if that was necessary. And it didn't even occur to her to ask first.

Ben smiled. "Everything checks out."

Laura felt both relief and disappointment at the pronouncement.

"Isn't that good news?" Shelly asked.

"Of course." Laura needed to focus on something else. "Guys, do you mind if I borrow Shelly for a moment?"

"Sure," Aaron said, his eyes questioning.

"Just girls' stuff," she explained.

Laura strode away from the men, assuming Shelly would follow. Hearing footfalls on the linoleum, she was right. They stopped near a window back toward the elevator. This section of the hallway was deserted. Laura poked her head into the nearest room and, seeing it empty, pulled Shelly inside.

"I need to talk to you," Laura said. She inhaled deeply. And didn't say anything.

Shelly quirked an eyebrow. "You need to actually speak for this to work. Is it about what you asked Ben to check for?"

"No, it's not." Laura wasn't ready to talk about her magical issues yet, but she had another issue that Shelly was uniquely qualified to weigh in on. "You know Aaron and I have been looking for a house. For me," she added when she realized how that sounded.

"Yes."

Laura stared over Shelly's shoulder. "I realized today that I've been delaying choosing one."

"Not because you couldn't find the one you like?"

"Yes and no."

Shelly laughed. "That's not really an answer."

"I mean, no, I didn't find one that I liked. But." Laura bit her lower lip. "I kept changing what I told Aaron I was looking for."

"You didn't!"

"Well, that's not accurate. I kept increasing what I wanted. Yeah. That's more accurate."

"That seems logical, to be honest. The more homes you see, the more you realize what you want."

Laura glanced out the window on the far side of the room. "True."

"Except that it's more than that," Shelly guessed.

"He asked me on a date," Laura blurted out, then averted her gaze.

"You said no?"

"I work for his mother and we're work colleagues."

Shelly shook her head. "Those aren't reasons. It's a small town; everybody works for or with someone's family. And he's only finding you a house. *He's* not your boss."

"What about if it's because I liked Ben before? That's weird, right?"

"Yes, it's weird that you're using that as an excuse. Because, no, it's not at all weird to like one person years ago and someone else now," Shelly said. "Besides, I thought you moved on from high school." Shelly added this with a knowing look, and Laura flushed at having her own words tossed back at her.

"It's not weird that I liked Ben before and now I find Aaron attractive?"

"Not at all," Shelly repeated.

Relief swept over Laura. Intellectually, she knew that

there was nothing wrong with liking one brother years before liking the other. But, emotionally… She needed to hear someone else say that it was no big deal.

"Besides, I took Ben off the market, remember?"

"Indeed," Laura said and impulsively threw her arms around the smaller woman. "Thank you."

"You're welcome."

"Sorry if that was awkward," Laura said. Although that made three hugs in one day. She was acting all out of sorts today.

"No need to apologize. It's nice to see this—" Shelly paused. "—softer side of you. Human."

"Oh." Laura didn't know what to say to that. She never really had friends before. Maybe this was what that felt like.

"Don't worry, I won't make it more awkward," Shelly assured her with a laugh.

"Thanks." Laura glanced at the room's exit. "Let's join the men and find out if this John Doe is our missing owner."

CHAPTER FOURTEEN

AARON

"What do you think they're talking about?" Aaron asked nervously, wishing he could be a fly on that wall.

"Relax, little brother." Ben glanced down the empty hall in the direction the women had gone. "I don't hear yelling, so I don't think they're fighting or anything." He grinned. "Or are you worried they're talking about you?"

Aaron's eyes widened. "Why would I think they're talking about me?"

"Oh, I don't know. There's some wicked chemistry between you two."

"There is?" Aaron swallowed. "Yeah, there is. Except I asked her out and she said no."

Ben pursed his lips. "Give her time. She'll come around."

"I hope so."

"That's not what you came here for."

"No, it's not. Is this the John Doe's room? And he looks like the photo I sent you?" Aaron asked, indicating the closed door behind Ben.

"Yes, to the first question. And a strong maybe to the second."

"What happened to him? I know you're not supposed to talk about his medical condition with me, but maybe it'll help us identify him."

"Oh, yeah, I wouldn't be doing this if not for the fact that we're making zero headway with him."

"What do you mean?"

"A concerned citizen found him wandering a few blocks from here."

"Near the house that's for sale."

"Um, not too far off from that. The town's not that big, though, so that could be said about almost anything."

Aaron laughed. "Touché."

"He has some facial contusions suggesting a fight or accident."

"What did he say when you asked him?"

"We didn't. By the time he arrived here, he was delirious. We started treatment immediately, of course, and now we're just waiting for him to wake up." Ben lifted the chart from its holder next to the door and scanned the top.

"What's his prognosis?"

"Pretty good. I expect him to wake up sometime today. His vitals show he's responding well to the treatment."

"I guess that means the police haven't found his family yet."

"No, I assume not—"

"I need to give this name to the police," Aaron interrupted. "His family must be worried sick."

"Maybe see if you agree that he looks like the same guy," Ben cautioned, "before you notify the police and give a potentially worried family false hope."

"I see what you mean." Aaron brightened. "There's another option."

"There is?"

"Ginger can tell us."

Ben was well-aware of his brother's magical inclination, so didn't bat an eye at Aaron's idea. "If she's not in surgery, yeah, she probably could. Regardless of his facial bruising, she'd recognize his smell."

Aaron saw the women approaching in his peripheral vision.

"What have you been talking about?" Shelly asked, all wide-eyed innocence.

Ben smothered a laugh, and both Aaron and Laura turned beet-red.

"We were just about to go in and see John Doe," Aaron said into the awkwardness.

"That's a great idea," Laura said with more enthusiasm than the situation warranted. She opened the door and walked between the others to stand by John Doe's bed.

Aaron, Shelly, and Ben were a moment behind her. Aaron took his phone from his pocket and opened the photograph of Marvin Kelm.

The bruises, wires, and oxygen mask complicated their review, but in the end, they were confident it was him. His legs stretched to the bottom of the bed, so he was tall. His shaggy black hair fell in lank pieces around a face with slight wrinkles. He appeared to be the same late 30s or early 40s that Marvin did in his profile photo. The fall of the sheet suggested he was a little plump, maybe like an athlete gone soft.

"Is he going to be okay?" Laura asked, her heart breaking for the likely Marvin and Ginger.

Ben walked the women through the background and prognosis he'd provided to Aaron.

"Since we think it's him, what do we do next?" Shelly asked.

Ben and Aaron exchanged a look.

"I had an idea." Aaron explained the plan to bring Ginger to the hospital, sneak her into this room, and then she could identify whether the man in the bed was her owner.

"That's brilliant," Laura said, and Aaron warmed at the compliment.

"Is Ginger okay to be picked up?" Shelly asked.

"I was about to check." Ben typed into his phone and within a minute, a response arrived. He winked. "The vet okayed her to travel. She didn't need surgery after all."

Aaron grabbed Laura's hand without thinking. She curled her fingers around his. "You ready to go get our dog?"

CHAPTER FIFTEEN

LAURA

Go get our dog. Warmth flooded Laura at Aaron's choice of words and the fact of his fingers entwined with hers. They were in this together. On an adventure to help someone. She'd missed this feeling of closeness with someone else. *Not since my parents—*

Thankfully, they reached Aaron's Jeep before she could follow that thought. This time he drove the short distance to the veterinary office. As they parked, a text dinged on Aaron's phone.

"It's my mom," he explained. "She wants to know how Ginger is doing."

Laura grinned. Esther really had a big heart.

Aaron typed a response, then frowned at the reply.

"What?" Laura asked.

"She's asking how our lunch went." His ears turned red as he typed. "I'm explaining we ate at your desk while we found Ginger's owner."

Laura didn't know what to think, so she nodded and waited for him to finish.

Aaron put his phone in a pocket and then they headed for the vet. He held the door open for her and they entered the foyer.

"Hey Aaron," the receptionist greeted him when they entered.

"Hi Shannon," he said. "We're here to pick up Ginger. I believe my brother called?"

"Yep." Shannon picked up the phone. "Can you bring Ginger up?" She flashed a smile at them then hung the phone up. "It'll just be a minute. By the way, she has a microchip. When we scanned it, it didn't have current information. The person we called said they gave her to a rescue. They didn't remember which one. And she hasn't been a patient in this office before."

"Okay, thanks, Shannon. That's helpful."

Laura hung back, watching the easy conversation between Aaron and Shannon. He was so personable. She doubted he had any frenemies. Laura almost laughed at the rambling nature of her thoughts, but stopped short when another technician appeared, leading Ginger out on a leash.

The cute cocker spaniel had a bright orange wrap on her leg and a small shaved spot, where maybe they had to give her fluids. She seemed happy to see them, wagging her tail and offering quick little barks.

Aaron chuckled. "Yes, Ginger, we're here to bring you to your owner." He kneeled before her. "Is his name Marvin?"

Ginger barked.

Laura had no idea if it was a confirmation until Aaron said, "Yes."

"We're going to bring you to him to confirm, okay?" Aaron asked the cocker spaniel.

Ginger barked again and both the receptionist and technician looked on as if this were the most natural thing in the world. As if every day, someone spoke Dog in their office.

Of course, this was Wildcrest. Maybe they did see this more often.

Aaron scratched Ginger behind the ears again, and her wagging tail wiggled her entire body. He stood and accepted the leash from the technician. "Thanks."

With that, the three of them returned to the Jeep. Aaron secured Ginger in the backseat. Laura giggled when he pulled the seatbelt over her. It was necessary, but she wondered if the dog would stay put. Then Aaron explained to Ginger that she needed to stay put, and Laura understood.

"That's handy," she said.

"What is?"

"Being able to tell an animal what you want them to do."

Aaron slid into the driver's seat and smiled at Laura. "It's not always that easy, but when I can share a simple picture of her in the seat with the word *Stay*, that has a higher likelihood of success."

"I love it," Laura said.

"Me too."

They stared at each other, the air heavy with promise. Laura licked her lips and Aaron's eyes dilated.

"We'd better get Ginger to the hospital," Laura said shakily. She couldn't remember the last time she'd kissed a man, and the thought saddened her.

Aaron gripped the steering wheel. "Of course."

The short drive back to the hospital remained expectant. Laura wondered what it would have been like to kiss Aaron at that moment. Butterflies took flight at the thought and she concentrated on settling them.

He parked the Jeep without comment, and let Ginger out of the backseat.

"She moves well with that flexible cast," Laura commented.

"It was just a hairline fracture. Shouldn't take too long to heal," he said. "Ben told me," he added, at her questioning look.

The trio walked to the side of the main entrance and considered their plan.

"Ben obviously knows we're doing this," Aaron said.

"But the hospital doesn't allow dogs?" Laura asked.

"No. What do you think?"

"Are therapy dogs allowed?"

"Maybe," Aaron answered. "There's only one way to find out."

They shared a conspiratorial grin, then waltzed into the hospital.

"May I help you?" a woman at the front desk asked, staring back and forth between them and Ginger.

"We're here to visit Marvin Kelm," Aaron explained.

"This is Ginger, our therapy dog," Laura added, with an air of complete confidence.

"Oh, okay. Do you know where you're going?"

"Yep. Dr. Benjamin Wright provided the room number," Aaron said.

The receptionist visibly relaxed at the chief resident's name, and Laura wondered if that might get him in trouble later. She hoped not.

"I hope the patient enjoys the visit," the receptionist called out as they headed toward the elevator.

"That was fun," Laura admitted while they rode the elevator up to the third floor.

Aaron nudged her with his shoulder. "Rebel."

"You know it."

The elevator doors opened and the trio walked down the hallway to the closed door of Marvin's room.

"Let me text Ben that we're here and headed in."

While he did, Laura crouched at Ginger's level and scratched her behind the ears, rubbing the velvet softness. The dog rewarded her with a lick on the cheek.

"She likes you," Aaron said.

"What's not to like?" Laura quipped.

"Indeed."

Laura reached for the doorknob. "Moment of truth," she said.

It was obvious they had the right man the instant they entered Marvin Kelm's room. Ginger began dancing around, offering quick, happy barks. She swiveled her head back and forth between Aaron and Marvin, the latter sleeping in the bed.

"I'll wake him up," Aaron assured the excited dog. "Hold on."

Ginger sat on her back haunches at Aaron's words.

"Mr. Kelm? Marvin?" Aaron approached the bed. "We have someone here who'd like to see you."

Marvin didn't respond. Aaron continued to speak softly to Marvin and then switched focus. "Ginger?" The cocker spaniel cocked her head in response. "I need you to bark, but as quietly as possible. Can you do that?"

Before Laura could voice her question, Aaron answered. "She understands what I'm telling her, I promise."

Laura chuckled. "I believe you." She watched with rapt attention.

Ginger padded closer to Marvin's bed. When her rump hit the floor, she emitted a tiny yip.

Marvin's eyes fluttered open. "Hello?" He rasped the question. His eyes focused on Aaron and he licked his lips. "Hello?" he repeated.

"I'm Aaron. You're in the hospital. We found someone who belongs to you." He leaned down and picked up the wiggling dog.

"Ginger!" Marvin tried to sit up further but floundered among the wires.

"You might want to use the bed controller," Laura suggested, hiding a smile at the obvious delight of both Marvin and Ginger at being reunited.

Once Marvin adjusted the bed to be seated upright, Aaron carefully set Ginger in his lap. They showered each other with kisses while Aaron and Laura watched.

"Thank you," Marvin said to them, tears of gratitude in his eyes.

"You're welcome," Laura and Aaron responded together, eliciting a chuckle from all three.

"What happened?" Laura asked.

Marvin explained he hadn't been feeling well a couple of days ago, and had run out of supplies to check his sugar levels. Stupid, he knew. So, he tried to manage it without checking. He realized that wasn't working and so tried to drive himself to the hospital. He was so unaware that he hadn't even noticed Ginger jump into the back seat before he closed the car door. Unfortunately, he must have blacked out, because he drove into a tree. What happened next was a bit of a blur, he said. He remembered fragments of walking on the street, then getting into someone's car and being brought there.

"I was so worried about Ginger, but couldn't find my words to express it." He sipped at the water by his bed. "I can't thank you both enough for bringing her back to me." He glanced at a meal tray. "If only I had orange Jell-O instead of green," he joked with a tired smile.

Aaron laughed dutifully at the attempt at levity, though Laura beamed.

"I might be able to do something about that," she said with a wink.

"You can?"

Laura grabbed the Jell-O off the tray. "Be right back."

Aaron followed her out of the room. "Are you doing what I think you're doing?"

"Yep." Standing outside of the room, with Aaron shielding her from the view of interested eyes – although the hallway was empty – she held the container in her hands and concentrated.

Laura imagined the green dessert as orange. She tasted the flavor of sun-ripened oranges in her mouth, pictured the bright orange of a tangy gelatin. The air above the container grew hazy and the color fluctuated. She could do this. There was nothing wrong with her magic.

The fruity concoction resembled a rainbow, a chaotic mix of green, orange, blue, and red. She frowned. That wasn't supposed to happen.

"Is everything okay?"

Laura heard Aaron's voice as if from a distance. She concentrated harder, but it was like before with the parking lot blacktop. The air grew hazy a second time and the colors swirled. Until they stopped.

"It's not supposed to be brown, is it?" Aaron asked.

"No, it's not." Laura stared at yet another failure of her magic. She couldn't imagine what was happening. Nothing had changed—

The moments with Aaron. She'd almost kissed him twice. Right before each instance of her magic going haywire. There couldn't be a connection.

Could there?

CHAPTER SIXTEEN

AARON

Aaron kept wanting to say something to Laura, but the thought of saying the wrong thing stopped him each time. They were on their way to Laura's house. Ben had agreed to keep Ginger in his office until Marvin was discharged; as Chief Resident, nobody would enter his office uninvited.

Aaron pulled up in front of her current house. "We solved the mystery," he said, and she offered him a slight smile in response.

"We did. What should we do next?" she asked.

"Since Marvin's awake, he can let his family know he's okay. I guess I'll work on the offer you want to put on the earlier house. Sound good?"

She stood outside the Jeep, leaning against the frame. "That sounds good. Let me know what you recommend for an offer."

"I'll have a draft this afternoon. Talk soon." That last was said to her back. She'd closed the car door already. She gave a half-wave over her shoulder and walked to her front door. He waited until she'd gone inside before pulling away.

During his drive home, his mind remained occupied with thoughts of Laura and her magic not working. Those thoughts still crowded his mind as he opened the door to the home he shared with his brothers. Although he figured Ben wouldn't be with them too much longer. Aaron couldn't imagine Ben and Shelly wouldn't have moved in together by the end of the year.

Aaron crossed through the open floor plan living area toward the three bedrooms in the back, pleased as always by how well their remodel of the home had gone. The real estate agent in him loved to highlight in his mind what he would put into a listing. *Quartz-topped kitchen island. Dark laminate wood flooring throughout.* He shook his head. They weren't looking to sell yet, that was certain.

His familiar, Elizabeth, stretched out on his black bedspread, barely visible with her sleek black fur. Until she opened her bright green eyes when she sensed him in the bedroom.

"What's wrong?" she asked.

He should have known his reincarnated great-something-or-other ancestor would know he was mulling an issue. As much as he could understand other animals, the connection to his familiar surpassed that communication and understanding by leaps and bounds.

Aaron sat beside her on the bed, stroking her fur. "I don't know what to do," he admitted. He summarized asking Laura out, her refusal, their almost kisses, and her magical fiascos. "I thought I just needed to wait out her resistance. She clearly has feelings for me. Then it hit me in the car driving home that her wacky magic happened after we had our moments." His voice softened. "Surely our feelings for each other aren't affecting her magic. Right?"

Elizabeth rolled over to sit in a perfect pancake pose, paws under her chin. "I wasn't there," she meowed, "so I couldn't say with complete certainty. But."

"What?" Aaron dreaded what his familiar might say next.

"If intimate moments—"

"They weren't intimate," he interrupted.

If a cat could roll her eyes, she probably would have. "You know what I meant. If emotional moments between the two of you preceded her magic not working properly, it may very well be that your magic isn't aligned with hers." Elizabeth licked her paws.

"We have misaligned magic?" His question dripped with dismay.

She stopped licking her paws. "It's possible."

"Can we fix it?"

"Not if it's truly misaligned. No."

Aaron laid back on the bed and stared at the ceiling. "If we get together, it may cost Laura her magic."

"It's possible."

"I can't do that to her. I can't hold her back like that." Aaron laced his fingers behind his head. What he liked to call his thinking position.

He considered that Elizabeth couldn't say for certain that his and Laura's magic were incompatible. Something else was possibly going on. It could have been a coincidence that her magic messed up after they almost kissed. But if they were misaligned? Aaron knew he couldn't be the cause of Laura not being able to use her magic. They'd joked about him asking her out again after she bought her house. That would never happen.

There was no way he could pursue her now.

CHAPTER SEVENTEEN

LAURA

The awkwardness topped the scale. Laura couldn't believe Shelly Newsome was sitting across from her in her own kitchen. It had been a tough call to make, but Laura knew she needed guidance.

"Walk me through what happened," Shelly instructed.

Laura did, explaining how her magic didn't work right after the two near-kisses with Aaron. "It can't be that, can it?" Laura pursed her ruby red lips.

"I've not heard of magic interacting like that," Shelly said, then frowned.

"What?"

"There was something…" Shelly's sentence trailed off.

Laura's stomach clenched. "What? What is it?"

"At the barbecue."

"When? Oh, right, the barbecue." Laura and Aaron had gone together to celebrate Litha. She rarely attended those events, but that was at the start of her home search and he'd encouraged her to go. "Wait. What happened at the barbecue?"

"I remember there being something off there."

"What did you notice? What was off?" Laura asked.

Shelly's brow furrowed. "The magic floating around was off."

"Whose magic?"

"I'm not sure," Shelly admitted, "but something was wrong."

"You could already sense our magic was incompatible?" Laura's heart broke. Shelly's magical inclination was an ability to see the order in chaos, and this extended to sensing the magic of others. If Shelly said their magic was incompatible, then that confirmed it. Laura should have known not to develop feelings for Aaron. So stupid.

Shelly reached for Laura across the dark brown kitchen table, thought better of it, and placed her hand between them on the wood. "Don't overthink it. That's not what I said."

"Then what are you saying?" Laura demanded.

"What I said," she responded lightly. "There was something off. Something about the magic seemed chaotic." Shelly offered a lopsided grin. "But remember, there are two caveats to that."

Hope bubbled up. "There are?"

"One is that you know my magic has a history of misfiring."

"I thought that had settled down once you identified your magic."

"Not quite," Shelly said. "I understand it more, for sure. But it still isn't always accurate."

"Oh, wow." That blew Laura away. She hadn't realized that Shelly's misfiring magic still misfired. "And you're okay with it?"

Shelly lifted a shoulder in a blasé shrug. "It is what it is. Would I rather it not misfire? Sure. But, it's not the end of the world. At least I know it better now. Plus, sometimes it's great."

Laura's mind swirled with that idea. Even if her magic was incompatible with Aaron's, maybe that would be okay.

"The second caveat is that there were dozens of people at the barbecue," Shelly continued. "Just because I sensed something off when I was focused on you and Aaron—"

Laura flushed at the idea of the two of them as somebody's focus.

"—doesn't mean it wasn't somebody else near you."

"And there were a lot of people near us," Laura finished the thought.

"Precisely."

"Ask him out," came a voice from the bay windowsill.

Laura and Shelly swiveled their heads toward Laura's familiar sitting in the sun. "The peanut gallery speaks," Laura said.

"What did Eddie have to say?" Shelly asked. Of course, she only heard the meow, not the words and images that came through for Laura.

"He said to ask Aaron out."

"Pretty good advice," Shelly said.

"Yes, it is," Eddie agreed, licking his front paw. "As always, you're overcomplicating things. Ask him out."

Laura laughed.

"What?" Shelly asked.

"He's agreeing with you." Laura considered the advice of both her familiar and her no-longer-a-frenemy. They were probably right. Her chemistry with Aaron was undeniable. His asking her out already made it clear he wanted to go out.

All she had to do was call him and ask.

"You're overthinking it," Eddie said.

Laura rolled her eyes and translated the meow for Shelly, who nodded in agreement with the tabby.

"Is there something else?" Shelly asked.

The uncertainty in the question hit Laura hard. She wasn't sure how to respond; while they were no longer frenemies, they weren't friends. But why weren't they? Because Laura had crushed on Ben in high school when all he wanted was Shelly? Because Laura had thought everything came so easily to Shelly?

"You're definitely overthinking things," Shelly echoed Laura's familiar.

"There is something else," Laura answered Shelly's question.

Shelly waited for Laura to decide whether or not to share with her.

"It's more than just possibly losing my magic. Although that would be huge."

"It would."

Laura swallowed past her dry throat. "I don't know if I can risk it again."

"Risk what?"

"Loss," Laura whispered, the single word barely audible, but sounding loud in the silence that followed.

Understanding dawned on Shelly's face. "Your parents?"

Pain flooded Laura. She had never known her grandparents; they'd died before she was born. But, her parents...

"You don't have to talk about it."

"I know." Laura's eyes burned hot with unshed tears and she blinked them away. "I thought they would always be there. I didn't think it would matter if I went away to college."

Now Shelly took Laura's hand across the table.

"They died."

"I remember when that happened." Shelly squeezed Laura's hand. "I'm so sorry."

"I left. And they died." It had been a thunderstorm during Nevada's monsoon season. An unexpected flash flood had wiped their car from the road, and them from Laura's life. "I don't think I could take another loss."

A tear slid down Shelly's cheek.

Laura yanked her hand from Shelly's and wiped at her own dry cheek. "People leave." There was no point in rehashing the memory.

"They do," Shelly agreed. "That's inevitable, to some degree."

A hysterical laugh broke through. "That's not making me feel better."

Shelly chuckled softly in response. "It's true, though. Part of the risk of opening yourself up to another is recognizing that they will eventually leave. Or you'll leave them."

"Why do it then?" The raw need in her voice startled Laura.

"Because life is empty without it."

Laura sat with Shelly's pronouncement. Her life was pretty good. She had a great job that she loved. Coworkers she liked. A familiar she loved. Even a rental she liked well enough.

But.

Having Shelly here, like a genuine friend. Experiencing a true connection like she'd felt with Aaron. She'd missed having those in her life.

Maybe Shelly and Eddie were right. Maybe she was overthinking this. Nobody could predict the future. Her magic might be just fine with Aaron's. And maybe they'd be soul mates, destined for decades together. A smile flitted across her face.

"You've decided."

"I have."

Shelly smiled. "Then my work here is done."

Laura walked to the kitchen island to retrieve her phone, then sent a text to Aaron.

Come over when you have the draft offer ready.

CHAPTER EIGHTEEN

AARON

Aaron smiled at the text. Laura didn't ask as most people would have. She stated what she wanted and expected him to agree or explain why he didn't. He appreciated her blunt style, so similar to his own. Disappointment rose at the thought they could only be friends, and he stamped it down. She was a great person. He'd count himself lucky to be her friend.

Laura's timing was perfect. Putting together the draft offer on the house had been easy enough. And he knew they would accept it. He'd recommend offering less than asking, since she was paying cash, and that was the true magic word with house buying. Aaron had been about to email the draft offer to her. Instead, he printed it out to bring with him.

The short drive to her current rental gave him time to steel himself for seeing her. He was resolute that he wouldn't be responsible for her losing the magical side of herself. If they couldn't be together, then he'd have to watch for and avoid opportunities to flirt.

How disappointing. Flirting with her had been so much fun. Maybe they could? No, he shut that line of thinking down. No matter how much fun she was; how much he enjoyed being challenged by her; or how beautiful, smart, and capable she was, he could never ask her to risk losing what it meant to be a witch. If she couldn't even make Jell-O a different color. No, his feelings weren't more important than the essence of who she was.

He almost threw all of his mental effort away when she opened her front door. Her short red hair, a little disheveled, which was unlike her, framed her beautiful pale face. And those lips. He didn't know the name of that color red, but it sure made her lips kissable.

Ugh. That was exactly what Aaron wasn't supposed to be focusing on.

Her smile becoming uncertain clued him into how long he'd been standing silently in her doorway.

He gave a quick shake of his head. "Sorry about that. I was thinking." He thrust the papers at her before she could ask him what he was thinking about. "Here's the offer."

Laura's azure eyes sparkled and she took the paperwork. "Wonderful. We can review in the kitchen."

Aaron considered the black furniture and stark white walls with no photographs. It made his fairly minimal furnishings appear downright decadent. Somehow, though, it worked for her. Sleek, sophisticated. More expected in a bustling city, maybe, than in a small town, that type of classy.

They entered the kitchen and Laura gestured to a tiny cat sitting on top of the dark brown kitchen table. "That would be Edward. Eddie. He's not supposed to be up there." Though she crossed her arms, her half-smile gave her away. This was clearly a game they played.

"Hi Eddie," Aaron said and the cat's uneven whiskers twitched in response. Aaron sat opposite Laura at the table. "Go ahead and read the offer, and we can go from there."

"Of course." Laura began reading the first page.

Aaron watched her read, wondering why it was taking her so long to finish the first page.

She placed her hand flat on the page and stared at him.

"Is something wrong?" His stomach flip-flopped the longer she looked at him. "Take a picture. It lasts longer," he quipped.

She snorted at the terrible joke, but that broke the tension. "Thank you for bringing the offer. I'll read it. However, first," she started. Laura stood from the table.

Aaron pushed back his chair to join her. "Laura?"

"I've given this a lot of thought, and I overreacted when you asked me out before. You were right that saying I couldn't date you because work connected us made no sense. So, I'd like to correct that." She paused her rush of words and offered a hesitant smile. "Would you like to have dinner with me?"

Yes! his brain shouted.

"No," his mouth said instead.

Laura appeared confused and her shoulders hunched for a moment. Then she straightened up to her full height, so that in her heels she was looking down at him. "My apologies for misunderstanding. Thank you for—"

"Don't you want an explanation?" Aaron asked, his traitorous brain trying to find a way to salvage the situation.

"You don't need to explain," Laura said. Then she crossed her arms again, before dropping them to her sides. "Actually, if you have one, that would be great."

"I do," he said, eager to explain. "It's not that I don't want to go out with you."

"I don't understand."

"It's that I don't think we're a good fit." He dropped his head back for a moment. "That came out wrong. When your magic didn't work right before, what did those events have in common?"

She walked to lean against the kitchen island, her back to him. "We almost kissed."

"We almost kissed," he repeated. Laura turned and Aaron was startled to see tears glistening.

"Do you think our magic doesn't go together?" she asked in a flat voice that made his heart hurt.

"I don't know," he admitted, "but Elizabeth thinks it's possible."

"Your familiar?" she asked, and he nodded.

"Elizabeth thinks there's something wrong. She wasn't certain, but she said we may have misaligning magic." He struggled to finish. "And that if we get together, you might lose the entire essence of your magic."

CHAPTER NINETEEN

LAURA

"Shelly said the same thing," Laura gasped. She escaped the closeness of Aaron to return to her seat at the kitchen table. *This can't be happening.*

"She did?" he asked.

"She didn't call it misaligning, just said something seemed off about us when we were together at the barbecue."

"At the barbecue? Oh, the celebration."

"Yes." She told Aaron what Shelly had said about the magic seeming off, instead of the typical orderly magic she felt. "She couldn't state it with certainty though because other people were around. So, I thought it was worth the risk. But now?" If her feelings were visible, they'd be ricocheting all around the kitchen, like the chaotic magic Shelly described.

All that potential hope that might have become love crashed into the despair and disappointment of having Shelly's words echoed by Aaron's familiar.

Aaron pulled a chair closer to her and took her hands in his. "But now?" he repeated.

His touch sent shivers of pleasure down her spine. She reveled in the feeling, and didn't know how they could ignore this connection when they were together.

When she didn't continue, he did. "I couldn't forgive myself if I caused you to lose your magical essence." His thumb rubbed circles in her palm.

"I know," she whispered. There had to be a way. "Maybe it's worth taking a chance. After all, neither was certain."

Aaron released her hands and sat back, almost as if he needed the physical distance between them to say what he'd say next. "You're right that they weren't certain. Elizabeth definitely said it was only one possibility."

"And Shelly said it could have been someone around us at the barbecue," Laura continued the line of reasoning eagerly. They could work this out, she just knew it. "Who was around us at the barbecue?"

He tilted his head in thought. "Members of my family and our friends were the closest, most of the time."

The unspoken *and none of yours* bounced around in her head, though she knew he didn't mean it that way.

"Except that nobody else was around in the parking lot when you made the pothole bigger," he said.

She flinched at his words, despite their neutral tone. He was only working through the hypothesis that she had proposed.

"And nobody except Marvin Kelm was around us when you tried to turn the Jell-O orange. I don't see how somebody else at the barbecue could be the cause." He opened his arms wide in helplessness.

Laura felt like she was trying to breathe underwater. He was right, of course. Nobody at the barbecue had been around them when her magic failed. She had been so sure they'd find a solution, some other explanation. It couldn't be that they had misaligning magic. The Goddess wouldn't be so cruel as to bring him into her life just so she had to choose between him and her magic.

"Tell me what you're thinking," Aaron said.

She hesitated.

"Please." He batted his eyelashes at her.

"You're such a dork," she said. But it worked and she smiled, albeit wistfully. "You're right."

"That doesn't happen every day," he quipped, still trying to break the mounting tension.

"It's going to be okay," she said, not sure if that was directed at him or herself. "I wouldn't want you to feel responsible for me losing my magic, either. That wouldn't be fair to either of us."

"I wish it was different," he whispered.

"Me too." Laura stood. "I'm sure the paperwork is great. I'll review it this afternoon." She started to leave the kitchen, Aaron jumping up to follow.

"Good. It's a great house. You'll look great in it." He flushed.

"Thanks," she said, her thoughts stuck on the idea that there had to be a solution or explanation that would allow her to be with Aaron.

"Ben asked if I could take Marvin and Ginger home from the hospital today," Aaron said as they stood in Laura's front entrance.

"I'm so happy they're going to be okay. That's nice of you to bring them home."

"What can I say? I'm a nice guy," Aaron said with an impish grin.

Laura grinned in return. "Yes, you are."

Aaron gave her a side-hug. "I'll see you later."

"Yes, you will," she whispered. Her resolution grew stronger.

This wouldn't be another confirmation of people leaving her. There had to be an explanation for why their magic appeared to be misaligning. She'd find it. Then she and Aaron could be together.

CHAPTER TWENTY

AARON

Aaron drove his Jeep too fast through town, finally exhaling when he reached the hospital. He needed the distraction of bringing Marvin and Ginger home.

Laura had asked him out. And he'd said no. Knowing she wanted him as much as he wanted her broke his heart. They'd just realized they both felt the same way. Including that a relationship wasn't worth losing a part of herself for. If only they'd found another explanation.

Aaron texted his brother. *Do you want to bring Ginger to Marvin's room? Or do you want us to pick her up on our way out?*

I'll bring her to you.

Aaron trudged to the elevator, still not able to leave his conversation with Laura behind. His spirits rose along with the elevator. It would be nice to help a man and his dog get back to their home.

Thus, a smile brightened his face as he reached the doorway to Marvin's room.

"Are you my ride?" The tall man sat on his bed, shaggy black hair sticking out in all directions.

"Yes, sir, I am." Aaron scanned the hospital room. "Do you need help with anything?"

"Nope," Marvin answered. "They gave me this fabulous outfit. Mine had some, um, stains on it."

Aaron considered Marvin's oversized t-shirt with the yellow smiling emoji and baggy jeans a few inches too short. "I suppose that's preferable to a stained outfit. Barely."

Marvin belly laughed, the skin at the corner of his eyes crinkling.

Commotion at the door drew both men's attention.

"Ginger!" Marvin practically lunged for his dog, who gave him sloppy kisses in return.

"Thanks for bringing her up," Aaron said to his brother.

"Just glad I could help." Ben glanced at his watch. "Perfect timing. I gotta go."

"A Chief's work is never done?" Aaron asked.

"Something like that." Ben handed the paperwork to Marvin. "Since you're following up with a private physician, I went ahead and completed your checkout. You're free to go."

"Thank you, Doctor," Marvin said solemnly.

"You're most welcome." And with that, Ben disappeared into the hallway.

"Are you two ready?" Aaron asked.

"Yes," Marvin and Ginger responded.

Aaron led them to the elevator.

"What am I taking you away from to be my taxi?" Marvin asked, Ginger trotting beside him.

An image of Laura flashed in his mind. "Nothing important." The words burned even as they left his mouth.

Marvin's dark brown eyes flashed with something like merriment. "I don't believe that for a moment."

Aaron's face flushed as the three of them entered the elevator. "Why not?" He tried deflection instead of answering.

"Are you asking why I don't believe you?"

"Yeah." Aaron stared at the elevator doors, willing the car to reach the ground floor.

"Because you're a terrible liar."

"Gee, thanks." Aaron cut his eyes at Marvin. "You know, I don't have to take you home."

"I know." The elevator doors opened and Marvin and Ginger stepped off first, with Marvin holding his arm out to let Aaron off, too. "But I also know you won't do that."

Aaron sighed. "No, I won't."

"I'm just playing, anyhow."

The trio crossed the foyer and soon were blinking in the bright afternoon sun. Aaron led them to his Jeep and got them situated before he spoke again.

"I know you're teasing," Aaron said with a smirk. "You're also not wrong. About any of that. Address?" He typed the address as Marvin recited it.

Once the Irish-accented voice on the GPS began, Marvin picked the conversation back up. "Sometimes talking to a stranger is easier."

"Sometimes there are things you can't discuss," Aaron responded.

"Is it related to how you can speak to and understand my dog?"

Aaron jerked the car over to the side of the road and hit his hazards. "What do you mean?"

"When you and the lovely lady brought Ginger to me, you communicated with Ginger. For-real communicated, not just empathetic-but-still-human guesses. I'm assuming the issue you don't want to discuss is something supernatural."

The statement was matter-of-fact, but Aaron probed the man's face for apprehension, disgust, or some other judgment. He saw nothing. "It is."

"Maybe related to the young lady, too?" Marvin asked in a sing-song voice.

"You're good," Aaron said with a laugh.

"It wasn't hard to see that the two of you have feelings for each other." Marvin lifted one hand from where it rested on his legs to point at Aaron.

"Alright. You've convinced me." Aaron pulled back on the road and drove exactly the speed limit as he spilled forth his tale of woe about misaligning magic.

Marvin remained silent when Aaron finished.

"What do you think?" Aaron asked.

"I'm collecting my thoughts."

After Aaron turned onto the next street, Marvin pointed out his house and Aaron coasted to a stop in front of it. Aaron shifted in his seat.

Marvin similarly shifted so the men faced each other. "It's a doozy, for sure. And unfortunately, unless you can find another reason for the misaligning magic, I think you're making the right decision to not pursue her."

Aaron's face must have reflected his misery on hearing Marvin's conclusion.

"Sometimes the best thing we can do for someone is to let them live their life," Marvin said, patting Aaron's knee. "Good luck. Thank you again for getting us home."

"Of course," Aaron responded, then helped Marvin and Ginger into their home, essentially on auto-pilot.

Everyone seemed in agreement. He and Laura likely had misaligned magic. And, without another explanation, letting her go was the best thing he could do.

But if that was so, why couldn't he accept it?

CHAPTER TWENTY-ONE

LAURA

The thought that she could find an answer to the mystery of her magic misaligning with Aaron's buoyed Laura's energy. She'd considered calling Shelly to meet her at Wildcrest Wizardry for an afternoon coffee, but she ran into an even better possibility before she could do so.

"Hi Laura. It's good to see you," Grace Newsome greeted Laura when they crossed paths in the checkout line. The supernatural life coach stood next to her youngest daughter, Patricia, who went by Patty. The older Newsome wore her typical long flowing skirt, and the younger wore jeans and a concert t-shirt.

"Hi Grace. It's good to—" Laura started to reply then

stopped. Seeing Patty, who Laura thought was away at graduate school, gave her an idea.

Grace quirked an eyebrow. "It's good to what? I think you're missing part of your sentence there." She stepped up to the counter before Laura could respond. "Hey Mom."

"Hey Nana," Patty added.

Laura watched tiny Grace stand on her tiptoes to hug her equally short mother on the other side of the counter. Grace's parents had owned the apothecary and coffee shop for years. Laura stared at the back of Grace and Patty's heads as they placed their orders. When the two turned and stepped aside to allow Laura to order, she reached out a hand to stop them.

"Do you have a few minutes?" she asked.

Grace squinted her purple eyes. "I do. I can see you need help."

Since Laura was a recent client of Grace's life coaching, she knew the comment wasn't malicious. "Thank you."

"Mom, I can catch up with you later," Patty said.

"Actually, would you mind staying too?" Laura asked.

Patty's hazel eyes widened at the question. "Um, sure."

Laura placed an order for a double shot espresso, her usual, and the three women sat at one of the handcrafted wooden tables.

"How can Patty and I help?" Grace asked.

"How come you're in town?" Laura asked Patty instead of answering Grace.

"I'm on a break from grad school. And you're deflecting," Patty said.

Laura reddened. "Guilty." She picked nonexistent lint from her dress, then laid her hands flat on the table. "How can you help? I'm not sure. Grace, your insightful thoughts are always helpful. But, Patty, you're the one I think I need more." She took a deep breath and then shared all the recent back and forth she'd had with Aaron. Patty was nodding by the time she finished.

"I can see why you wanted my help," Patty said.

"Sorry to interrupt, ladies, here are your coffees," said a voice over Laura's shoulder, before she could reply to Patty. Rebekah, the tall, bubbly, blond manager of the store, leaned over to distribute their beverages.

They murmured their thanks and Rebekah withdrew.

"Do you think you can?" Laura asked eagerly. She knew that Patty's magical inclination was like the other women in her family: she was in touch with the magical energy of others. Specifically, Patty read the magical energy of witches as if they were auras. She could see if there was anything wonky going on. If anyone could alleviate Laura's concerns, it was Patty.

"I can tell you that nothing stood out about you or Aaron's magical auras at the barbecue," Patty said.

"Thank the Goddess," Laura said in a rush.

"But," Patty continued, "I get what my sister said. Even though I didn't notice anything off about your magical auras, there was some funny energy floating around that day."

"Was anyone else's magical aura off?" Grace asked her daughter.

Patty sipped her coffee. "I thought maybe I saw something, except when I looked closer, it wasn't what I thought."

"That was clear as mud," Grace said, laughing her deep-throated husky laugh.

"Whose magical aura was it?" Laura asked.

"I can't answer that," Patty answered.

"But what if that person is related to mine and Aaron's misaligning magic?" Laura heard the desperation in her voice and she didn't care. This was too important.

Patty placed her hand over Laura's on the table between them. "I understand you want answers. And I wish I could give them to you. But I don't know for certain what I saw. Plus, either way, it wouldn't be my information to give."

Intellectually, Laura understood. Emotionally, she hated that Patty wouldn't tell her.

The younger woman smiled sympathetically. "You said there wasn't anybody around you either time your magic didn't work correctly, except Aaron. The likelihood that this other person I saw at the barbecue being involved is therefore pretty small." She patted Laura's hand. "If it makes you feel any better, right now when I look at your magical aura, it looks clean and bright. No issues. Believe it or not, it could have been a coincidence that your magic didn't work in those two instances."

Relief flooded Laura. Of course. Coincidence. How did the saying go? Once is a chance. Twice is a coincidence. Three is a pattern. Maybe they just needed to test the theory. Her face flushed at the thought of almost kissing Aaron again.

"I can see you liked that news," Grace said drily.

"It does make me feel better," Laura admitted. The thought that she and Aaron could have a chance thrilled her.

"For what it's worth, I don't think your magical alignment is a problem. Even if it is..." Patty shrugged. "It could be temporary. It could be permanent. I still say if you like him, go for it."

"Really?" Laura looked at Grace, who nodded in agreement with her daughter. "I'll think about it."

And the next time I see Aaron, we'll test the theory that it was a coincidence, Laura thought to herself, biting back a grin.

CHAPTER TWENTY-TWO

AARON

"Hey, Mom, yeah, I'm waiting for Laura now," Aaron said to his mother, who'd called him right as he'd unlocked the front door. With a glance around the house, he decided to wait for Laura at the desk staged in the front den. That way, he'd be close to the door when she arrived. He smiled at the thought of seeing her.

"Does that mean you're finally going on a date?" his mother asked.

Aaron sat on the edge of the desk. "No, it doesn't," he said. His mother sighing in response didn't make him feel any better.

"That's a shame," Esther said.

"I know, but you know what the issue is."

"There has to be a way around it."

"I appreciate your enthusiasm, Mom, but I really don't think there is." Saying the words out loud made them seem more real. His throat tightened and he coughed to clear his throat.

"I love you, son." Her voice sounded thick with emotion.

His eyebrows lifted. Although he knew she felt that way, his mother wasn't the touchy-feely type to express it randomly like that. "Love you, too, Mom."

The doorbell rang. His heart rate galloped like a wild horse.

Aaron hopped off the desk and rushed to open the door. "Gotta go, Mom. Laura's here." He ended the call before opening the door.

Laura stood in the doorway, appearing uncertain, though still commanding with her height and demeanor. Her personality filled every space she was in, but he saw her softer side, too.

"Thank you for asking the listing agent about my seeing the house one more time before putting in the offer," Laura said.

"Of course," he responded. The sunlight glinting off her red hair mesmerized him. Ugh, he knew he shouldn't think like that. "Is there something specific you wanted to see?" Despite his internal emotional wrestling, he was a professional and could focus on that. He stepped aside so Laura could enter.

"No, nothing specific," she said, strolling around the main open floor space.

"Really?"

"That surprises you." She giggled as she continued to walk, almost aimlessly, but wound up in the kitchen.

His mouth dropped open, and he snapped it shut before she could see – right now, she was staring down at the kitchen's quartz countertops – and that's when it hit him. She seemed happy, yet nervous. It was an unusual combination. Almost like first date nerves. Which this wasn't.

"Um, yeah, I guess it does," he said. "I'm used to you being pragmatic." He leaned against the counter. "Wanting to come here without a specific purpose seems out of character."

Her eyes met his, her expression sober. "Is that a bad thing?"

"Not being pragmatic?" Aaron found the entire conversation bizarre. There had to be subtext he was missing.

"Being out of character," she clarified.

"I like your character." Aaron couldn't believe he'd said that. His palms felt sweaty. Now he was the one acting like this was a first date. That he was failing miserably. Of course, they weren't on a date. They'd decided to just be friends. If only his heart would accept what his brain had decided. In truth, what he and Laura had decided together.

"You do?" she asked.

The coquettish tone in her voice threw him and he went bold. "You know I do. I asked you out," he reminded her with a smirk.

"True. Except then you said no when I asked you out." She stepped closer to him.

Aaron fought the desire to cross his arms as a physical barrier between them. She was confusing him. He'd thought they'd decided to just be friends. To protect her magic.

Laura took another step closer. A kaleidoscope of emotions crossed her face and she sighed, almost imperceptibly.

"What?" he asked. The naked fear on her face shocked him. If only he knew the cause.

She shook her head. "Maybe later," she mumbled before offering a wide smile that didn't quite reach her eyes. "I don't really need another tour. Let's discuss the offer we want to make on the house." She pulled the paperwork he'd brought her out of her leather bag.

The whiplash change of topic hurt his brain, but she obviously was working through something. He suspected it involved him and he wanted desperately to ask.

But their misaligned magic had thrown her, so he withstood the barrage of his own emotions to give her space to work out her own. He knew she'd tell him when she was ready.

Based on her ping-ponging emotions, he figured he didn't have long to wait.

CHAPTER TWENTY-THREE

LAURA

Laura saw that their conversation was confusing Aaron. That made sense since her own mind was a whirlwind of thoughts and emotions. It was time to present her plan. Except Aaron had accepted her topic change and was talking.

"Of course, we can skip the tour and discuss your offer. Their listing agent said they're expecting another offer on the house, given the limited availability in Wildcrest."

Laura frowned. The home was perfect. She would do whatever it took to get it.

"I wouldn't worry about it, though. Your all-cash offer will be hard to beat, even coming in below list."

"Are you sure?" She bit her lower lip.

"I can't guarantee it, of course," he said with a grin, "but cash is king, as they say."

Her ability to present an all-cash offer was bittersweet. Yes, she'd saved a lot while working. That was easy to do when you did little outside of work. But, she had more than was typical for someone her age because of the deaths of her parents. Between the life insurance and the sale of her parents' home, she had a full bank account.

A wave of sadness crashed over her. She'd give all of it back in an instant if she could have her parents alive and well.

She offered a shaky smile and ignored the concerned look on Aaron's face. "That's wonderful. I'd like to make this offer," she said, indicating the paperwork, and then put it back in her bag.

Aaron checked his watch. "I'll text the listing agent she'll get our offer tonight. She'll most likely present it to the owners in the morning. I suspect they'll accept or counter by the end of the day."

Hope flared. "But not a rejection?"

"I'd be shocked if that happened." Aaron quirked an eyebrow. "Then everything will turn over to the title company and I'll be out of your hair."

Her heart lurched at the thought. "Maybe not," she blurted out.

"No?" he asked.

Laura couldn't read his neutral face or the inflectionless word. *Time to go for it.* "I have an idea."

"You do?"

She paced to the living room's sliding glass doors, hearing Aaron's footsteps on the hardwood floor as he followed. The view of the desert and low mountains beyond calmed her. Laura faced him.

Aaron had stopped by the staged beige couch. He'd remained on the far side of it. To give her space?

"It's possible that our magic isn't misaligned."

A cautious smile surfaced. "It is?"

Laura nodded. "It is. It may have been a horrible coincidence that after we shared, um, emotional closeness, my magic didn't work the way it's supposed to." She swallowed past the lump in her throat.

He gripped the back of the couch. "What makes you think that? That would be great if it's true."

Laura explained what Patty had said about her magical aura looking clean. "So I'm proposing a test."

"What kind of test?"

"We recreate an emotional moment, and then I try to use my magic. We see what happens." Her effort to maintain an objective tone failed.

Aaron's eyes dilated. "And what would this emotional moment look like?"

Her face flushed and she waved in the couch's direction. "Let's have a seat."

They sat, not touching, though with their knees only inches apart. "Now what?"

She reached a hand toward his face. "I'm not sure," she admitted.

His hand captured hers. "This seems like it's going well."

Laura exhaled and tightened her grip. She was hyperaware of the softness of the couch's fabric under her other hand, the mild musk of his aftershave, and the sound of the wall clock in the kitchen ticking off the seconds.

He leaned in to kiss her.

She jolted back.

"What?" he asked and released her hand.

"Sorry about that. We've never kissed before." Oh, but she wanted to!

He grinned. "There's always a first time."

"That wouldn't fit the parameters of our experiment."

Aaron chuckled. "Fair enough."

"I think I should try to use my magic now." Fear coursed through her. *What if it fails?*

"You can do it," he encouraged her.

"Thanks," she responded shakily.

"What do you want to change?"

Laura glanced around the room, feeling relief as the intensity of their closeness faded to tolerable levels. That had to have been enough emotional closeness for the experiment.

Her gaze landed on a staged flower on the coffee table. A beautiful yellow rose. Signifying friendship. "I'm going to change that yellow rose to red," she told Aaron.

"Go for it," he said, then shifted slightly away from her, again presumably to give her space.

She sat up straight, keeping the yellow rose in her vision and creating a representation of it in her mind. She concentrated on changing the yellow rose in her mind to red. It began to shift from yellow, the familiar haze appearing above and around the physical rose.

The haze shimmered. Splotches of pink appeared on the rose. Almost like it was being tie-dyed. The pink spread and darkened. Happiness filled Laura as the rose became redder, almost matching the richly red rose in Laura's mind. It was working.

Pink reappeared. The haze wavered. Soon the physical rose resumed its tie-dyed look. And there it stayed.

"No," Laura whispered, devastated by the failure of her magic and what that meant. Three failures were a pattern. She looked up to meet Aaron's face. His expression of dejection no doubt matched her own. "That's it," she stated.

"I don't know what to say," Aaron responded, reaching for her hand again, before dropping it onto the couch.

"What is there to say?" Laura asked sadly. "We tested the coincidence theory. And we proved the theory false."

"That's it," he echoed her.

Laura choked back a sob. "I'm just not ready to accept that I won't be able to have functioning magic anymore."

"I understand." He half-smiled. "I couldn't ask you to do that, either. But I suppose I'm glad we tested the theory."

"No questions left unanswered," she said.

"Exactly. No regrets," he added.

Laura couldn't agree with him. She had plenty of regrets. Or to be more accurate, she wondered if this would become a regret.

CHAPTER TWENTY-FOUR

AARON

Aaron sat slumped on their shared gray couch in the living room when Ben walked in, though Aaron didn't acknowledge his brother.

"Earth to my little brother," Ben said and flicked the back of Aaron's head. It had been the brothers' greeting since they were kids. It was done with love, and not enough force to actually hurt.

But it got Aaron's attention and he stood up. "Hey big brother. How's the hospital?"

"Fine. How did it go with Laura today?"

Aaron snorted. "You've been talking to Mom."

"I have," Ben admitted with a shrug. "Since you didn't

say anything about Marvin, I assumed you got him and Ginger home safely."

"I did. Sorry, I forgot to text."

"No worries." Ben smirked. "That leaves seeing Laura. Do you need a glass of wine to talk about it?"

"Sure, why not?" Aaron agreed and followed his brother into the kitchen.

"Mom didn't seem thrilled," Ben said, grabbing glasses and a bottle of red wine.

"No, she didn't." Aaron perched on one of the high stools at the center island. "I know she's always advocated for Laura, but her interest in this seems weird." He accepted a glass from Ben. "Thanks."

"Of course," Ben replied, and they both sipped their wine. "Ah, that's good. As for Mom, yeah, I don't know. She definitely likes Laura. Maybe she sees something you two crazy kids can't see." Ben's eyes twinkled.

"Don't start. You know that's not the issue."

"I know." His expression softened. "What happened?"

Aaron brought Ben up to speed on Laura's hypothesis, and how it bombed.

Ben appeared thoughtful. "Interesting."

"Not really," Aaron disagreed. "Her magic failed again after we…" he trailed off.

Ben waved that away. "I realize that. This time seemed different."

"What do you mean?" Aaron cupped his wine glass.

"You don't see it?"

"Obviously not."

"What was different that time compared to the first two times?"

"I'm not one of your medical students," Aaron warned. "Don't Socratic Method me."

"Mea culpa," Ben said with a laugh. "The third time, it almost worked."

Aaron ran through the three events in his head. Ben was correct. "It backfired at the very end. What do you think it means?"

Now Ben shrugged. "That I don't know. But I suspect it's not as clear-cut as you and Laura are treating it. Patty could be right about it not being permanent. Maybe it's already adjusting," he suggested.

"Hmm, that *is* interesting. I hadn't thought about it that way." A light appeared at the end of the tunnel. "I wonder if I can convince Laura to see it that way."

"It's not about convincing her of anything," Ben cautioned.

"Oh, I know. Bad choice of words. Besides," he said and smiled wickedly, "I don't believe anybody has ever convinced Laura to do something she doesn't want to do."

Aaron needed to show her that she wanted to be with him, and that she wasn't risking her magic. He picked up his phone and texted her.

"I'm going to need the room," he told his brother.

"Good luck." Ben topped off his wine glass. "I'll leave the rest of this for you."

Aaron hoped he'd need it to celebrate and not to drown his sorrows.

His phone dinged an incoming text.

I'll be right there.

CHAPTER TWENTY-FIVE

LAURA

The turquoise front door shined in the waning light of the early evening. It was gorgeous. Aaron was gorgeous. Laura bit back a laugh at how quickly her thoughts had gone there. It confirmed the decision she had made. She pressed the doorbell, listened to the short chimes inside the home.

"Thank you for meeting me here," Aaron greeted her.

Laura smiled at his disheveled hair and untucked shirt. He really unwound at home. "Of course, you beat me to it. I was about to text you."

"You were?"

He appeared so hopeful that she knew she was doing the right thing. Following her gut. "I was." She smiled shyly.

"Please come in. Would you like some wine?"

"Definitely," she answered while they walked through his beautiful home.

"Please have a seat," he said, gesturing to the stools lining the island.

She almost smiled at the formality. *Is he nervous?*

"I'd like to discuss something with you."

"Can we talk?"

They asked their questions simultaneously and laughed.

Aaron handed her a glass. "I hope red is okay. And, please, ladies first."

Laura accepted the wine, gulped a large swallow, and organized her thoughts. "I like you. As more than friends," she added.

If her bold opening startled him, he didn't let on.

"And the fact that we both asked each other out confirmed mutual interest." She didn't know why she was acting so formal.

She rolled her shoulders back and breathed deeply. "I don't like that we have misaligned magic. And, maybe the others are right, that it's not misaligned. Or that maybe it is, but it won't be permanent."

Aaron sipped his wine, his eyes never leaving hers.

"Regardless, I don't care."

He almost spat out his wine. She laughed as he brought a hand up to his lips to make sure he didn't dribble any.

"I'll figure that out as we go. We only live once. And I

can't speak for you, but it's not every day that I have such a connection with someone."

"It's not every day for me either."

Laura stood from the stool and walked around the island to Aaron. "So, if you haven't been put off by this craziness, and you're not worried that our misalignment will affect your magic—" She took his hands in hers. "—I'd like to ask you out again."

"Before I answer…"

Worry spiked through her and she tightened her grip. "No, I must insist you answer the question first."

His eyes crinkled with a smile. "Technically, you didn't ask a question."

"You should have been a lawyer," she said, though she relaxed her grip. "Would you like to go out with me?"

"Yes, I would," he said.

Her heart fluttered with happiness and she leaned toward him. Their lips met. *Who knew such a blunt, fast-talker would kiss so sweetly?* The feelings of closeness and connection filled her heart. She knew she sounded like a romance novel, and that was okay. This was why people read them. Whatever was happening with her magic, they'd work it out together. This. This was what mattered.

He pulled back with a smirk. "But I do want to say something."

"After a kiss like that, you can say anything," she whispered.

Aaron told her about his conversation with Ben, pointing out what she had also missed about the difference with their magic test.

"He's right," Laura gasped. "How could I have missed that? That truly does suggest some other factor at work, or the temporary nature of the misalignment."

"It does."

"I'm so glad," she said with a sigh of relief.

"Either way, we'll go through it together," he said, almost verbatim echoing her thoughts.

Laura knew for certain at that moment. They had their happily ever after.

EPILOGUE

AARON

Laura's hand entwined with his brought Aaron so much pleasure. They had arrived in the backyard of his parents' home to celebrate Lammas, the first day of the grain harvest. The coven enjoyed celebrating the seasonal sabbats, and since the focus was on grain, various baked goods covered the folding tables set out around the spacious backyard for the afternoon's celebration. Everything was decorated in red, orange, brown, and yellow, and Aaron saw goblets for wine and apple cider.

"So glad you could make it," Ben greeted the couple.

"Sorry we're late," Laura responded. "It's my fault. Aaron was helping me move furniture."

Aaron squeezed her hand. She'd been so happy when she closed on her new home. And to be there at every step had thrilled him.

"No need to apologize. I like having excuses to tease my brother." Ben nudged him with his shoulder.

"Whatever, old man."

"How're things going?" Ben asked, his tone serious.

Aaron knew what he was asking, and deferred to Laura for how she wanted to handle it.

"It's been mixed," she admitted. "Sometimes my magic does what I want it to do. Sometimes it fails. And sometimes it does something unintended."

"That sounds like my magic," Shelly said, hooking an arm into one of Ben's. "Mine misfires all the time."

Laura smiled ruefully. "I'm focusing on the good over the bad, and hoping that one day it'll work itself out."

"That's a positive approach," Shelly said. "Uh-oh, we're about to have all three brothers together."

"That's outstanding," Noah said, joining the two couples. "We're like Superman, Batman, and Spiderman."

"Hey, wait, let me guess, I'm the kid," Aaron objected.

"I think it's more like the three musketeers," Laura said.

"At least then they're all for one and one for all," another voice chimed in. The group turned to see Patty Newsome, in a flowered shift dress, her short dark hair held in place with a flowered headband. She joined the group and Aaron couldn't help but notice how she and Noah snuck glances at each other from the corners of their eyes. *Hmm, maybe there would be another Wright-Newsome union one day.*

"There's Mom and Dad," Ben said, interrupting Aaron's musings. "It must be time for the ritual."

The group made their way into the center circle, offering greetings to the other members of the coven encircling Elijah and Esther Wright. Aaron, as always, was struck by how downright regal his father was. He made a great coven High Priest.

"Welcome to our home, everyone," Elijah's deep voice rolled over the participants. "For Lammas, the first grain harvest of the year, we celebrate the fertile soil, remain thankful for the food on our tables, and we ask the Goddess for continued abundance, so that none may go without.

"Stalks of wheat, pieces of bread, and a small section of corn on the cob should be making their way around to you." He started the procession by handing those to Esther and saying, "I pass this gift of the first harvest to you." Elijah waited while voices rose and fell with the passing of the wheat, bread, and corn until everyone had them.

"As you consider the wheat you hold in your hands, consider the power of the planet we call home. Allow pieces of the stalk to fall to the ground as an offering, and remember that the power of the harvest is within each of us. The smallest seed can become the largest bloom. We each will send our roots to bloom and flourish.

"Now, consider the bread remaining in your hand. We are blessed to have this bounty."

Aaron repeated the phrase, the expected call-and-response of the ritual, before the group ate the bread pieces.

"Now consider your ear of corn."

Aaron smelled the richness of the barbecued surface of corn, his mouth salivating at the prospect.

"This corn represents the fruition of your intentions. See your intentions as part of a cornfield full of ripening corn. As you bite into your corn, remember what you offer for yourself, the coven, and the wider world."

Aaron watched Laura nibble at her corn, but he took a huge bite. The corn's juices flowed over his lips and he considered where he was today. The seeds he had planted professionally, within his family, and romantically, and how they'd come to successful fruition.

"May the love of friends, family, and the Goddess stay with you always." Elijah led them through closing the elemental gates and releasing the circle.

"And now we drink," he concluded, and the group laughed.

"Oh my," Patty whispered.

Aaron turned to her, as did Shelly, who stood on her other side.

"What?" Shelly asked.

"It can't be," Patty murmured to herself.

"Sis, talk to us," Shelly said.

Patty's gaze swung between her sister, Aaron, and finally came to rest on Laura, who narrowed her eyes at the scrutiny.

"I have a theory." Patty spun around and strode away from the larger group of coven members. Aaron, Laura, Shelly, Ben, and Noah followed, exchanging confused glances. Once Patty was beyond earshot of the group, she stopped. Her eyes shone. "I have a theory," she repeated. "About Laura's magic."

"Wait, what?" Laura asked.

"You do?" Aaron asked, flabbergasted that they might, at last, understand the misaligning magic.

Patty glanced around at them. "Remember what I'd said about the barbecue?"

Aaron knew Noah would be the only one who hadn't heard that. "I'll catch you up later," he whispered to his oldest brother.

"I didn't want to say anything because it had happened so fast, I wasn't sure of what I saw. Then, I didn't want to say anything, because I didn't feel like it was my story to tell if what I saw was true."

Laura grabbed Aaron's hand, and he hoped for her sake she was about to get some answers. Shelly looked like she wanted to shake her sister to get her to get to the point.

"But," Patty said. "Based on what I'm seeing now, I think it's okay to tell you because I think we may need to work together."

"On what? What are you talking about?" Shelly asked.

"I don't think you have misaligned magic." This Patty directed at Laura and Aaron, who both sighed in relief. "This will come as a shock. I think Esther is causing the magical malfunctions."

Dead silence for a moment, and then overlapping comments and questions came fast and furious. Aaron couldn't keep track of who said what.

"How do you know that?"

"How can Esther be the cause?"

"Esther doesn't have magic."

Patty shook her head.

The group quieted in anticipation. Aaron couldn't believe what Patty had said. His *mother* caused his and Laura's misaligning magic.

"At the barbecue, I saw an aura around Esther."

Shelly gasped, but it took Aaron a minute to understand.

"She shouldn't have a magical aura?" he asked, and Patty nodded.

"It flashed on and off so quickly, I thought maybe I'd hallucinated it. Even though that had never happened before," she said, with a glance at Noah, who dropped his gaze.

"What did it look like?" Ben asked, and Aaron almost laughed. Of course, Ben would be more interested in analyzing the *why* and *how* of it all.

"Chaotic," Patty said with a frown. "But again, it was gone so fast, I couldn't be sure. Until today." She stared across the backyard to where Elijah and Esther were chatting with other coven members. "While Elijah conducted the ritual, colors appeared around Esther. A magical aura."

"Oh, my Goddess," Shelly whispered.

"Exactly," Patty said, nodding sagely.

"But my mother doesn't have magic," Noah said.

"Except that can't be true," Patty argued. "Not if she has a magical aura."

"You must be mis-seeing or misreading, or something," Noah insisted. "She's middle-aged. Magic always appears at puberty."

Patty lifted a single shoulder. "I don't know what to tell you. She has magic. Whether she's always had it, or it's recently manifested, I have no idea."

"What does that have to do with my magic?" Laura asked.

"Esther's magical aura is chaotic. There's a very good chance it could affect the magic around her. You work with her almost every day."

"It doesn't seem to be affecting anybody else," Noah pointed out.

"As far as we know," she corrected, and he dropped his chin in a brief show of deference. "As I said, it's a theory. And something we should definitely talk to her about."

"Mom would be horrified at the thought of this happening," Aaron said. "I doubt she even knows she *has* magic, let alone chaotic magic."

"That makes sense," Ben agreed.

Noah nodded at Patty. "You're right. We need to talk to her about it."

Aaron looked around the group as they echoed Noah's sentiment. This had been an eventful Lammas. His mother apparently had chaotic magic now. And Noah and Patty clearly had some kind of *something* happening between them.

The year was shaping up in quite interesting ways.

Don't miss Noah and Patty's road to happily ever after in **Love's Misbehaving Magic (Wildcrest Witches, #3).**

And if you're wondering about the references to Las Vegas and the acceptance of the paranormal, turn the page for more on that completed series!

PARANORMAL TALENT AGENCY

Lights, Camera, Action (PTA, #1)

Welcome to the Paranormal Talent Agency!

When empath Catherine Rodham moves across the country to launch the west coast arm of the Peterson Talent Agency in Las Vegas, her plan goes awry when an actress on a film she helped cast turns up murdered, leaving law enforcement stumped.

Alex Moore, a Sin City actor with a secret, wants agency representation from Catherine – and maybe something more. But everything changes after he finds himself the target of a murder investigation.

When the two team together to solve the serial murders, Alex introduces Catherine to a paranormal underworld she never knew existed. Can Catherine prove Alex's innocence before losing her heart… or her life?

PARANORMAL TALENT AGENCY

Reset to One (PTA, #2)

The Paranormal Talent Agency Saga Continues

All vampire Evie Jones desires is to enjoy her fun immortal life as an actress. Until she meets fellow actor Ryan Walter, who intrigues her with his insistence that his best friend has been framed for murder.

The appearance of her movie producer ex-husband in Sin City complicates Evie's offer to team with Ryan to find the real killer. She wants nothing to do with her ex, but he may hold the key to more than one murder.

Amid their growing attraction, and with the help of her Paranormal Talent Agency friends, can Evie and Ryan solve the murders…and find their happily ever after?

PARANORMAL TALENT AGENCY

That's a Wrap (PTA, #3)

Mid-Season Finale of the Paranormal Talent Agency

Mia Fynn, a nixie who has lived among humans for over 200 years, loves her life as a producer in Sin City. When the lead actor in her upcoming movie is murdered during a live social media video, Mia finds herself thrust into the role of detective.

Jacob Dawson, an actual Las Vegas Metro Police Department detective, would rather not have Mia's assistance. But even he can't deny the literal sparks that fly whenever they touch.

With the help of her Paranormal Talent Agency friends and one nosy television reporter, Mia scrambles to catch a killer… and reel in her own true love.

PARANORMAL TALENT AGENCY

An Unexpected Sequel (PTA, #4)

Mid-Season Premiere of the
Paranormal Talent Agency

Five years ago, a desperate witch made a pact with a demon. Now Robin Landon, the owner of Landon Talent Agency, splits her time between managing the actors she represents and laboring as a demon's minion.

When Robin refuses the demon's order to kill Jackson McKee, a witch with a day job as a camera operator, she must balance her growing feelings for the intended target and evading the vengeful demon's wrath.

Out of options, Robin turns to her former nemeses with the Paranormal Talent Agency. Will their daring plan save Jackson from the demon, or will Robin lose both her chance at love and her life?

PARANORMAL TALENT AGENCY

Jumping the Shark (PTA, #5)

The Penultimate Episode of the Paranormal Talent Agency

Demon Barbara Knollman enjoys her reign as the head of Las Vegas and barely tolerates the necessity of running for office. But when her precognitive abilities save her from an attack on the candidates, she becomes both target and suspect.

Uncertain of her next steps, Barbara agrees to help angel Liam Collins stop a supernatural being hellbent on taking control of the paranormal world by whatever means necessary. And wonders if she's heading down a path of no return.

Accused of murder and with her demonic powers on the fritz, Barbara allows Liam to convince her to team with the Paranormal Talent Agency. Can Barbara clear her name, stop a killer… and open her dark heart to true love?

PARANORMAL TALENT AGENCY

The Season Finale (PTA, #6)

The Exciting Conclusion
of the Paranormal Talent Agency

Television reporter Elizabeth "Liz" Addison is investigating the supernatural story of a lifetime. Except she doesn't know *what* it is, just *who* it is – Catherine Rodham, owner of the Paranormal Talent Agency.

Liz knows she's on the right track when a time-traveling ghost warns her that she'll die if she continues the investigation. She ignores the threats until her romantic interest in Antonio "Tony" DiMaio, the were-panther owner of *Soprannaturale*, puts him directly in the supernatural line of fire.

To save Tony and uncover the truth about Catherine, Liz and the Paranormal Talent Agency join together for one last wild adventure in the paranormal world of Las Vegas!

THANK YOU!

Thank you so much for supporting my work and reading this book.

If you liked the book, please consider leaving a review online.

Just a few lines would be great. Reviews are not only the highest compliment you can pay to an author, they also help other readers discover and make more informed choices about purchasing books in a crowded online space. Thank you so much in advance.

If you didn't like the book or have concerns, please email me directly at
heather@heathersilvio.com

ABOUT THE AUTHOR

Heather Silvio mostly writes fun, fast-paced paranormal mysteries & flirty romance with guaranteed happily ever afters. She sometimes strays from that to write non-supernatural fiction, and even the occasional nonfiction book. Heather is also an actress and clinical psychologist who channels her inner flapper as a 1920s jazz and blues singer when she isn't working.

Visit https://www.heathersilvio.com for more information and to sign up for her weekly newsletter.